Backyard of
Corpses
Narratives from Kashmir

Backyard of Corpses

Narratives from Kashmir

SYEDA AFSHANA

PARTRIDGE
A Penguin Company

Partridge books may be ordered through booksellers or by contacting:

Partridge India
Penguin Books India Pvt.Ltd
11, Community Centre, Panchsheel Park, New Delhi 110017
India
www.partridgepublishing.com
Phone: 000.800.10062.62

For Abbu Ji and Ammi Ji,
the proud parents of
dearest Zubair,
my great support.

Special thanks to Fayaz Ahmad Kaloo,
Chief Editor *Daily Greater Kashmir*

TERMS

Aaj Tak—	Indian Hindi News Channel
Aamad-i-bahaar—	Arrival of Spring season
Ajnabi—	An Indian telefilm starring villain Danny Dengzongpa
Akhbaarwalla—	Newspaper Vendor
Alkatrass—	Prison on Island Alkatrass
Arizal—	Name of a village in Central Kashmir
Avtar—	A new personification or aspect of a continuing entity
Azaadi dil ki—	Freedom to be . . .
Azaan—	The Muslim Call for prayer
Balyaar, madanwaar and lolenaar—	Beloved one
Banihal Pass—	A Pass across the Pir Panjal Range at 9,291 ft maximum elevation. This mountain range separates the Kashmir valley in the Indian State Jammu and Kashmir from the outer Himalaya and plains to the south
Bishnois—	The tribe of people found in Central India and staunch believers of environmental conservation
Brazania—	Pun for land of brazen people
B4U—	Bollywood for you
Chai pani—	A bribe, not "tea and water" as literally translated

Chengaiz Khan—	Was the founder and Great Khan *(emperor) of the* Mongol Empire known for massacres of civilian populations for his expansionist designs.
Chinar—	The Oriental plane tree, native from southeastern Europe to northern Iran; found in Kashmir and popularly called 'Kashmir Tulip Tree'
Chinkara—	The Indian gazelle
Cinkara—	The energy drink brand name of Hamdard Laboratories Company in India.
Danny Dengzongpa—	An Indian Bollywood actor who usually played a baddie
Doonga—	Houseboat
Durbar-move—	Name given to bi-annual exercise of shifting the secretariat and all other government offices from capital city to another in the state of Jammu and Kashmir. It involves housing offices from May to October in State's summer capital, Srinagar and rest six months in its winter capital, Jammu. The tradition was started during Dogra rule in 1872 by Maharaja Ranbir Singh
Farmayish—	Request
Hari-Parbat—	Name of hill overlooking Srinagar
Halaku—	A Mongol ruler who conquered much of Southwest Asia. He was a grandson of Chengaiz Khan.
Hartal—	Shutdown

Hasti—	Self
Hazratbal—	Muslim Shrine in Srinagar on the banks of Dal Lake
Hindustani—	A popular patriotic soap of Indian Television
Hindukush—	An 800 km (500 mi) long mountain range *that stretches between* central Afghanistan and northern Pakistan
Izhar—	To express
Jannat of Shadaad—	Paradise of Shadaad
Jawahar Tunnel—	A tunnel under Banihal Pass used for road transport since 1956
Kalimah—	Declaration of faith by Muslims
Khabr-i-zaina kadal—	A famous vernacular newspaper column of veteran journalist late Khawaja Sanaullah Bhat, meaning 'News of Zaina Kadal'. Zaina Kadal is an old bridge in downtown area of Srinagar
Kuch kuch hota hai—	Title song of Bollywood movie made in 90s
Kuin ki her ek friend zaroori hota hai—	'Every friend is important', jingle of Airtel telecommunications
Line of Control—	(LOC) refers to the military control line between the Indian and Pakistani-controlled parts of the former princely state of Jammu and Kashmir—a line which, to this day, does not constitute a legally recognized international boundary but is the de facto border

Malkhah—	One of the biggest Muslim graveyards in the downtown area of Srinagar
Mantra—	Liberating the mind
Maslaki jung—	Intra-sectarian ideological clashes
Masti—	Mischief
Masval—	Kashmiri name for Iris flower
Mera bharat mahan—	'My India is Great', a patriotic campaign slogan
Mohallas—	An area of a town or village; a community:
Muezzin—	Person who says Muslim call for prayers
Naidyar Yarbal—	Series of steps leading down to a body of water
Nar hutun kazil wanus—	Title of poetry book in Kashmiri language written by Farooq Nazki
Naya ghar—	New home
Nayak to khal nayak—	From Hero to Villain
NDTV—	New Delhi TV (Indian News Channel)
Nikkah—	Nuptial knot of Muslims
Nimazees—	Muslim worshippers
Nishat—	A terraced Mughal garden built on the eastern side of the Dal Lake
Parampara—	Tradition
Pari mahal—	Named 'The Fairies' Abode', *is a seven terraced* garden *located at the top of* Zabarwan mountain range

Pheran—	A loose gown worn by people in Kashmir, traditionally, during winters to provide warmth and comfort while going about their daily chores
Pir-panjal—	A group of mountains that lie in the Inner Himalayan region, running from east southeast to west northwest across the Indian state of Himachal Pradesh and the disputed territories comprising Indian-administered Jammu and Kashmir and Pakistan-administered Azad Kashmir
Power ka sawaal hai—	Question of power
Punit Issar—	Popular Indian TV actor and director
Rainawari—	One of the oldest areas of Srinagar situated along the banks of Dal Lake
Ramzaan—	Islamic month of fasting
Rangeen—	Colourful
Rasm-e-chahrum—	Fourth day death ceremony
Rigveda—	Holy scripture in Hinduism
Saif and Salman—	Famous Bollywood male actors held in controversy over alleged killing of wildlife
'Salamun-Kowlun-Min-Rabin—Raheem'—	"Peace," a word from a Merciful Lord (36:58 Holy Quran)
Sangam—	A bridge where river known as Veshav is joined by Jhelum river in Kashmir
Sapnoo ki basti—	Dream land
Sattara, gaffara—	A commoner in Kashmir

Shikara—	Boat
SLR—	Self-Loading Rifle
Soth—	Bank of water bodies
Sumo—	A sports utility vehicle (SUV), manufactured by Tata Motors commonly used as a taxi in Kashmir
Surah—	Means 'Chapter' in Holy Quran
Surah-Al-Baqarah and Surah Yaseen—	Name of the chapters in holy Quran
Tantra—	A style of religious ritual and meditation that arose in medieval India
USP—	Unique Selling Point
Vindhyas—	A range of older rounded mountains and hills in the west-central Indian subcontinent
Vitasta—	Sanskrit name of River Jhelum
Waza—	Traditional Kashmiri cook
Yantra—	Sanskrit word for "instrument" or "machine"
Yeh dil maange—	An advertising slogan coined for Pepsi. It combines Hindustani and English, and literally means 'This Heart Desires More'
Yemberzal—	Kashmiri name of flower Narcissus
Zaina kadal—	Bridge in the downtown of Srinagar
Zabarwan—	Mountains that stretch on the sides of Dal Lake

CONTENTS

"You must have heard Rizwan was killed.
Guardian of the gates of Paradise.
Only eighteen years old . . .
From windows we hear grieving mothers,
and snow begins to fall on us, like ash.
Black on edges of flames,
it cannot extinguish the neighbourhoods,
The homes set ablaze by the midnight soldiers.
Kashmir is burning" . . .

Agha Shahid Ali
'The Country Without a Post Office'

CONFLICT

1

BED NUMBER 13

She was a pretty girl of fifteen, shy and reticent. Nature had brought her up in its lap. Green meadows and lush pastures had lent colour to her life: blooming with rosy hopes and dreams. Lofty mountains and alpine trees in the village had taught her way to measure heights in the world. Floating clouds and raindrops composed a dancing symphony for her. The wind would wriggle her stumpy feet, laughing in her artless face. The nesting birds made her feel the warmth of sharing. Brooks and rivulets running along the thatch home whispered vivacious syllables to her.

She enjoyed every moment of her carefree 'microcosm', imbibing the subtlety of unimaginable essence. She never felt the need of giving tongue to her words, speech to her silence or eloquence to her smiles. Life simply drifted her like a morning breeze sweeping over the tender hearts of spring tide fields:

This wayward virgin girl is shy
Of speaking in front of strangers
Hidden by the veil
Of her vague expression
She passes by
Her head bowed
Ever so quietly.

But then, her sprightly coyness wasn't everlasting. Nature played its Law. And the law was furious one. The grey afternoon arrived. There were no rainbow colours around. Sun had lost the refulgence and moon returned to reclusion. Days were bloated with precarious shadows. All heartstrings had stopped the fluting. She was shifted to City Hospital.

It was an abrupt transition. From lush of a small hamlet to urban vileness. It was the world of faddish rat-racers and brainwashed zombies. Competition and compulsion were the hallmark of this place where people were obsessed with crossing finish-lines in a jiffy. It was a flashy world with quaint style of living. There was no visible sign of halt anywhere. A crowded ocean of hurried aims and objectives: all shallow and superficial. The people here wallowed in a linear thought. They saw life as a race. They had become running addicts, lured by the powerful metaphor of race, with its false promise of getting some place. They had lost the sight of the importance of staying in one spot and not chasing the fugitive sunshine. And they were paying a heavy price in terms of curdled brains and dead hearts.

It wasn't the *City Of Joy* ala Dominique Lapierre's paean of love and hope. It was a loveless and hopeless place haunted by ruthless shiftiness. A compost of derisive deceit and delirium : the devil-may-care city.

She was dazed and dumbstruck for she belonged to the category of people who reject the pseudo-adventure of the road and do not traffic in traffic. She belonged to those who knew how to relax because theirs is the way of the turtle and the snail: theirs is the spirit of Walk, Do not Run; of Stop; and Halt. She came from the place where grass grew under her feet and tickled, and nobody was bothered about it.

In the General Ward of the hospital, she would hark back to her roots in reverie. Something was corroding her inwardly. Her simpleton and poor parents would only gaze her anaemic face and morbid eyes. She was restless and fidgety. The apple of their eyes, their only daughter wasn't all right.

Doctors couldn't diagnose her disease for she gave a confused history about herself. There was total uncertainty in her voice. Perhaps she wasn't adept in words, and maybe out of sheer gullibility she couldn't reveal everything to strangers. All the medical investigations nullified her symptomatic illness.

One morning, when doctors on round arrived at her bed, it was empty. She had left the hospital against medical advice. Doctors knew the reason of her disappearance. The late night report of patient's ultrasonography was known to all of them. They were in a state of shock, tightlipped and tormented. They silently passed the empty bed number 13 and moved on with their routine. A bitter and bare truth was lurking in their minds. They wanted to discuss the case but something prevented them.

A week later, there was a referral call from Intensive Care Unit (Surgical) about a septic patient. The doctor-on-call from general ward was taken aback. It was a ghastly comedown : the patient was the same girl. She was in coma. Her parents were shattered. The doctor examined her and remained there for a long minute without hope, unmoving, his eyes still fixed on the gullible face of the young girl.

In the next second after that long minute, she was gone. Her pulse drowned in the sea of oblivion. Like a flicker of light she had vanished with doctor's eyes full on her, but without actually seeing even a premonitory wing beat. She was gone straight into that towering emptiness of masked truth which none bears to penetrate. For another long moment there was silence. Then from somewhere a cry came ringing down. Her parents had started wailing over her death.

She was young and had seen little of the world. She was awfully ignorant. Or, perhaps helpless too. She couldn't save or protect herself from the rage of shame. What is love; what is lust; what is good; what is bad; what is permissible; what is prohibited—it was all Greek to her. The ignorance cheated her and the poverty snatched her life. A beast had robbed her of her chastity and a quack had rived her body. She died of failed abortion.

The innocence on bed number 13, incognizant of ill-omened numeracy, was soaring painfully above the skies of her scenic landscape, flitting from peak to peak of the summits over there, searching out the devil who had sneaked in and stained the virgin jade of her habitat. In a harsh and wild medley of questions, she continued to strike and echo against the pinnacles of the Valley. Her people had proved too relaxed. They had stopped and halted passively over all things. It was a criminal silence!

Perhaps, her cry goes forever somewhere in to those upper regions, beyond the pretentious probity of her plunderers, who swear by the high religion and sin by their beastly instincts.

Perchance, it was good for her to die!

2

THE DEAD END

It was difficult to salvage the memory. There were different characters. There were different stories. The collective amnesia had inflicted everyone I saw around.

Watching the passing people and people pass, the drama of life and death seemed intriguing. I noticed an old couple, their eyes gleaming with a tapering eagerness. I saw a wailing mother, thinking of an appalling tragedy that has befallen her. The son she had lost had fluttered into oblivion. She was sobbing, "He's gone."

Unmindful of the truth in her words, I tried to stretch my hands to bring back down to earth the memory of his loss. I asked myself—"Is he really gone forever? Gone even from our thoughts?" For the fluttering was so gradual that the disappearance seemed a chimera.

I peered into the Dal Lake that used to buzz with vim and vigour. Its clear waters chanted the mirth of immaculate stories. I never knew it has gone dry and is gasping. The majestic hotels along the Boulevard never disclosed the cleft between nature and man. Sun always beautifully set over the mole hills as *Zabarwan* overlooked the tender drama in the air. The unfurled coloured curtains of still *Shikara* on the parched banks of Dal narrated the silent saga. Something was severely missing. I couldn't guess what.

I strolled through the heart of city. New shopping complexes and squall of vehicles confused me. I am not walking around American Mall Avenue. There is so much din and noise that I don't even hear myself. Whistles and horns break my reverie. Voices swallow me. Faces muddle me. Clueless eyes in the crowd tell me a tale without a title. I am looking for something.

The *Azaan* from the central mosque summoned the believers. I saw people sluggishly responding. The man with a long beard entered first, and he was also the one to come out early. He was a clerk in the nearby Government office where files hardly moved from one desk to other. The man to come out last was the fragile oldie who was the sweeper of the mosque and had lost his son in police custody. I stared him, searching for a word in his shriveled wrinkles. I couldn't.

I boarded the bus to reach somewhere. My destination wasn't obvious. I travelled to the last stop. The dead end. I found myself in a strange land where time was congealed and inmates were inert. They were cheery and yet gloomy. Loving as well as hateful. Religious and hypocrite both. Everything but alive. Life had taken a veiled recourse out here.

Men lived and still didn't live. The spirit of existence was absconding. Life had vanished slowly. It was a perfunctory breathing; a smothered wheezing. They mistook it as *Life*. They ate, slept and waked : mere survival decoyed their senses. Animals were not found in their territory.

With high aspirations and tastes lost, they were left intellectually debased. It was dust all over them. Everything was covered with it. It filled their existence; their world. In the middle of their Main Street, I saw a standing memorial that was shrouded in dust and cobwebs. I wiped the surface and found some peculiar words engraved on it—

"We pick up sand in our hand
And watch it trickle through our fingers . . . .
Our tears seep into it and disappear . . .
It encompasses us, This dust."

(N.M. Rashed, translated from Urdu
by Mahmood Jamal)

Dust filled my eyes. My vision blurred. But I could see the jaded wintry sun drowning in the cold murky waters of Dal. There was no *Maharaja* in the Grand Palace. No fairies in the *Pari Mahal*. *Zabarwan* was without green. The river flowing through my backyard had washed off everything. Blood. Tears. Emotions. Fear. Values. Faith.

O Gosh, I was in the familiar country! The majestic dome of Hazratbal Shrine gave me an allusion. The old couple I had seen in the beginning of my journey was in front of me. They were sullenly mute. However, the wailing woman was calm. She pointed towards the sky. I lifted my eyes and saw nothing. Even the vacuum was void. No song shivered in the air. The depths of darkness and despondency had snarled all. The memories of loss had flapped into oblivion. Life had gone for good. Death was overbearing. And memory had miserably failed. Forever!

3

BACKYARD OF CORPSES

I reclined on my barren banks after a hectic, depressive and disgusting period. I was looking towards the sky where I could see nothing but smog. My sight was blurred with the blood that was splashed on me. I thought to myself that was I really brought into existence to see this day.

I was remembered of the times when season was making a shift, from bone piercing cold to a pleasant summer. The night was illuminated. Clouds had given all way for stars to twinkle and moon to express itself. Nature was never cruel to me. I was made to originate from the beautiful mountainous region at the base of *Pir Panjal*. I also enjoyed the honor of being named by Ancient Greeks as *Hydaspes* that also happened to be the name of one of their gods. Having been mentioned in *Rigveda* as *Vitasta*, the holy scriptures of Indo-Aryans mentions me as a 'mark'. Also, King Jahangir in 1620, got impressed by my scenic look and ordered renovation of the spring of my origin in the shape of an octagon.

My course was made by nature in such a way that I nourished and fertilized many cities that came along my path. I used to be sparklingly lucid and quiet. A friend to all and a good listener, everyone used to express his anguish to me. I used to be an honest companion who would keep all their secrets. My patience and calmness used to be the source of inspiration for many people. My course was free. I used to flow in direction I liked. No divisions and boundaries ever divided me. It was in my nature not to be ticklish. I lived in peace and harmony with the people of all places and all shades of life.

The respect and love that I had for ages saw a gradual deterioration. This happened due to devilish human intervention. *Hydaspes* was walled off. *Vitasta* had to see its brutal divide on communal grounds. From my course to my discourse, everything witnessed a change, a downhill. My lush green shores were turned into virtual dustbins. Most of the drainage water was emptied into my strikingly clean waters. Once a source of inspiration, I was now regarded as the last abode of the ones who want to end their life. Paradox still exists, some jump into me to end their lives while some come to me to save their lives from greater dangers. Especially, when dogs chase them!

My course was barred. My path was diverted. Dams and barrages were built on me that ultimately turned me contentious.

My agonies did not end here. I saw mothers crying for their sons and sisters wailing for their brothers. I witnessed wives searching for their husbands and daughters mourning for their fathers. Unfortunately, it is me who harbors their loved ones. Some were thrown into me unnamed and some are buried unmarked on my banks. They were brutally killed and pitched into me. Disappeared are called they, but they appear within me. They are sleeping deep, down in my bottom.

I remain the backyard of corpses. I remain the backyard of stories. The backyard of subversion. The backyard of betrayals. My waters are coloured with sighs and screams. And lots of secrets I conceal, without affording to hide them further.

4

Bold Rizwan, Betrayed Rizwan

Adieu my mother, adieu!
Tear not your hair.
Dead I am not.
Around your lap,
Always will I be
Invisible, listening to
Those sweet songs
Which you had
Knit for my knot!
Adieu my father, adieu!
Though on last journey
I am
But first passenger
I am not.
O, father of martyr
Don't stagger
Alive I am,
Alive I will be!

Adieu my sisters, adieu!
Don't recall me
In hisses and sobs,
Back will I be
In your dreams
In your thoughts
To see you
In bridal apparel
With henna hands!
Adieu my friends, adieu!
Wipe out scalding tears,
Miss you can't me
For memories of
Shared moments
Will bind me
Close to you
To your hearts
Always!
Adieus and Adieus forever!

The novel renovation in the vicinity of his graveyard made no difference. The playing pack of boys nearby barely altered the poise of his resting place. The environs weren't that salubrious and breezy as the din of honking vehicles and clamour of walking pedestrians agitated the air. However, he was there, buried under the soil of his nation, listening to the voices all around.

Since so many days, his mother hadn't visited him. There were no fresh flowers on his grave. No soft fingers cuddled his epitaph. The melody of lullabies was missing. The touch of caressing hand was not there. So many painful memories raked up his soul. He had told her to bury him beneath her hearth when he dies; and cry for him whenever his dreams pooled in her eyes. Now, he guessed, mom might be busy in temporal affairs, trying to reconcile his irreparable loss with secret sobbing and sighing. She had, perhaps, gulped down the poisonous cup of awful pain . . .

> *"The blood dappled*
> *apparel of bridegrooms*
> *Is washed at the river*
> *by the mothers . . .*
> *The milky mothers pine*
> *And quiet*
> *flows the Vitasta."*

(Farooq Nazki *'Nar Hutun Kanzil Wanus'*)

He thought of his aged father. The dash of annoyance on his face was still haunting him. Father had never wanted his sole son to desert him in old age. Grief-stricken and forlorn, his support had crumbled down and he was shattered. He was struggling to prop up his family and carry along the spiky path of survival. Nonetheless, he was silently lamenting the death of his brave son. He was convinced that the son had engraved his name in the annals of history. His was a death—a death for a noble cause, he believed.

Sisters too were down in the dumps. Melancholic and mournful, they crave to hear him again and play pranks with them. Whenever the front door of corridor creaks, they feel he is in, calling each of

17

them by jovial nicknames. The bike in the garage was at a standstill and had gathered a thick cover of dust. For so long, none among them had a ride on it. The exams were near but he wasn't there to drop them at the exam centre in time.

Even his room was locked as mother had directed not to open it. All his belongings were intact and untouched. Sisters many a times tried to barge in, but a strange fear of facing the harsh and heartless reality stopped their steps. The dearest bro had disappeared somewhere into an obscure and enigmatic world.

Sudden sullenness sprouted in him. He was reminded of his affable friends, the ones who would even plough through his dreams and make him happy all the time. The mutual faith and fidelity had trussed them resiliently.

He had valiantly wrestled death with daring spirit and profound passion, losing the precious blossoms of his life. So many years have flitted away fretfully and frantically since then.

He lost his life those days when the fervour for right to dignity, that was vowed, made his countrymen hoist their voices audaciously. Everything was just spontaneous. Earnestly struggling for the liberty of their beloved homeland, which was never taken as an integral part of any formidable occupational force, the passion had dominated the mob psyche. The fervent populace had hailed everything blindly. The 'all-inclusive espousal' was demanding and rebellious.

But then, the things fainted and fizzled down, gradually. The *fears* grew dark and deep. The fear of endings; the fear of beginnings. The fear to die; the fear to live. Everyone failed to salvage the wings of the Spirit called Freedom. Everyone was tossed by fearful anguish and everyone missed *the spirit.* The sun bled the sky and gobbled it away ruthlessly. Forgetfulness swept all. The occupation had played its subtle artifice!

If only he knew! The scalding tears and shocking pain prick his soul. Lasting woe rip opens the scenes of betrayal before him. He shrieks bitterly, trying to come out of his grave and grab all by neck . . .

Flowing through the hearts
Eroding the barriers
Sliding into every mind,
The storm of Lethe
overtook all.
Eighty thousand souls
bulk of blood
pathetic cries
innocent tears,
It washed away,
washed abruptly! . . .
Nothing has happened,
nothing will happen.
Which Sacrifice?!
Whose Death?! . . .
Inconstant moods
Inscrutably unpredictable,
Infirm memory—
Unfold not tantrums

> But
> Indelible traits . . .
> Swim with the Lethe,
> Sell down the Vitasta.
> Follow waves,
> Forget graves
> forget evermore!

5

A PITIFUL PRISON

This is a distress call from a big beautiful prison. I am calling someone out there. Hello, is anybody listening?

I have with me thousands lodged in only one of its kind lock up. It is a prison that sprawls far and wide, with all house and streets falling under it. Everyone—old, young and children— have been imprisoned.

I and all others have become the mute followers of diktats. Diktats imposed from every side. We are sandwiched. Shutdowns and curfews. Stones and bullets. Decrees and laws. Criticism and victimization. There is no in-between. Anarchy sways.

I am stunned and shaken. Confused and cornered. Is it really a replay of 90's? The memories are still sharp and cruel. A shattering hailstorm of bullets and gory splitting of blood. Betrayals in the backyard. A crumpled history. Disheveled promises. And most poignant of all, the belied hopes wreathed in smudge and smoke.

This is *Kashmir*, then and now, cruising along through many a moon ago. Populace doomed to death and raspy moans giving way to shell shocked numbness bordering on disbelief. Kashmir continues to remain mired in obnoxious reality long after the headlines fade away. The eyes of evil; the hands of injustice; and the face of tyranny—all this gets immortalized.

Words tell stories, the facts and the details, the depth and the background. However, images evoke emotion and, more importantly, memory. We quickly forget the facts and details, the precise names, dates and places.

But we recall the images: the blood smeared dead bodies; the pedestrians fleeing a violent scene; the injured rushed to the hospital; the dwellings gutted into ruins; the vigil under the shadow of gun; the commonplace identification parades and cordons; the shutdowns and desolate streets; and much more.

Images in Kashmir always arrive with enough impact to leave a lasting impression whilst words land mostly with an intellectual whisper. Once a mother wailing over the corpse of her young son appears in print, she's everyone's mother. Once a begging orphan child is on the front page, he's everyone's child. Once coffins occupy a few inches of newsprint, they translate the blinkered past. Empathy is natural.

The *Washington Post* photo-journalists Carol Guzy loves to quote: 'Tell me, I'll forget. Show me, I may remember. Involve me, I'll understand.' Rightly so. During the last two decades, the lenses from Kashmir have brilliantly captured the resilience and remorse in the human spirit, even in the most dangerous situations.

Our Photo-journalists with cameras have voyaged into so many different souls and subjects. Their lensed pieces have proven to be historical documents and wistful reminders. Sometimes they really touch our very souls. And yes, at times, they make a difference. Perhaps a small difference to one person for one moment on one day, but meaningful nonetheless.

The lens men from here have always tried to catch and communicate their best. It may not fetch them *Pulitzers* but it has surely revealed their knack of photographic story-telling. And then, it's the people in the pictures and those who view them that are the important ones, and both perhaps testify their caliber.

However, their work so far has remained unacknowledged and disintegrated. That they ought to be duly encouraged, and their work preserved as a powerful witness and documented systematically by any autonomous body, makes a good proposal. Their frames deserve to be etched into permanent memory, for with their succour our posterity may easily discern the recycled death of Kashmir, hear its dying heartbeats, sense its last gasping, and mourn the loss of sense in a land where nothing goes beyond the experiments and expirations, the blusters and blunders.

As I write these lines, there is a slow bewailing in the neighbourhood about a young boy shot and battling for his life at Sher-i-Kashmir Institute of Medical Sciences (SKIMS). There is an eerie silence around after a violent ding-dong battle in the out street, the only real sign that tells it's not all okay.

I am again wordless, couched in a prison with the record of intangibles creeping in and the imagination sneaking out, as figures shelter a painful nostalgia between them. What consoles me are the words of Faiz's prison poem 'Evening' translated by Agha Shahid Ali:

> *Now darkness will never come—*
> *And there will never be morning.*
> *The sky waits for the spell to be broken,*
> *for History to tear itself from this net . . .*

(The Rebel's Silhouette)

6

A Singular Search

The rays of sunshine on the dew droplets hanging on white blossoms of almond trees, gave a look of pearls shinning on white gold. The fresh morning breeze that passedby, took away all elements of anguish, misery and suffering. The vast stretched mustard fields, touching horizon, gave a pristine look of life. The small stream gushing with icy water inspired new fate and direction.

Amidst these fields near the corner of stream, dwelled the janitor of these farms who was curiously waiting outside his hovel for midwife to announce good news. He alongwith his three little cute daughters was stressed. He was holding an unusual disquiet. "Congratulations! Your wife has given birth to a baby boy," exclaimed the midwife while coming out from the shack. The poor farmer at once rushed inside his hovel, and sat beside his wife and son. Tears started rolling down their eyes, and turning to heavens they thanked their Lord for bestowing unto them a son, after a long wait.

The mother was feeling extremely happy. She thought that she had now someone to help and take care in their old age. The sisters had got their brother now, one whom they would rely upon, besides playing and frolicking with.

Despite poverty being their burden, the parents decided to give their best to the son. The father started working overtime in other farms and the mother also began earning from yarning wheel. Both of them began to save money for providing quality education to their son.

Months passed by. Years flitted. The son continued studying hard and performing well. After some constant struggle, the parents saved some money. "We have some money; let us buy some piece of land. Then we may need to sell it for the marriage of our daughters and for the higher studies of our son" said mother to her husband. "That is a good idea, I really dream of my son becoming a professional". So they bought a piece of land to secure the 'certainties' of future.

One morning, the sun was fantastically bright. The blooms had manifested themselves in the shape of beautifully colourful flowers. The branches of fruit trees had bowed down due to clusters of fruits on them, and were in the offing of rich harvest. The golden looking paddy fields were all set to nourish and feed the farmers for their year ahead. The green trees reminded of serene prosperity. This was the day when their son got selected for engineering course in the city college. Their joy knew no bounds.

The young boy joined the course and put up in the college hostel. His parents never failed to visit him every month. They managed to bear the expenses of his study. The son also concentrated upon his studies and was ranked among the best students of the college.

Once, as a routine, he went to spend his post-exam holidays in his home village. The parents and sisters were glad to see him. Mother prepared his favourite dish for the dinner. Sisters sat around him and inquisitively inquired about the culture of city life, and the activities he does in his college. He chatted with them for hours, realizing deep down the responsibilities he had to shoulder for his sisters.

The day he had to go back, the sky was all cloudy and had entirely veiled the sun. The ambiance looked gloomy. The trees had shed their dried fragile leaves. The winds blew them aimlessly here and there. The son left his home and walked down the barren-looking fields, trampling upon the brittle leaves.

The parents had a sleepless night. Mother got scared with a sudden flash of lightning and thunder, followed by a terrifying cloudburst. It started raining heavily. "It is now two days since he left and we haven't heard of him yet; my heart is sinking" said anxious mother to her husband. "I also feel so, tomorrow we will go to see him" he replied.

Next morning, the air was foggy. The visibility was poor. They set out to meet him.

On enquiring about their son, they came to know that he has not returned to college so far. They were shocked. Frantically looking for any clue about him, they eventually landed in a police station. But it was all in a vain. Their complaint was not registered. They were harassed with a volley of irrelevant questions, and were told that few people had seen some armed men picking up a young boy in the vicinity of their village on the day when he had left his home. Who and how and why—the vagueness trapped them miserably.

Thus started a painful search—from every security camp in their district to all other prisons of the state, they ended up hearing nothing. It took them almost three months to look for him at various jails of the state. It drained them economically. The piece of land also went off in this ordeal.

They approached different organizations to help them in tracing their son, but felt they are getting exploited as their tragedy was 'sold' at various levels. The family was at crossroads. Penury and pain shattered them. Nobody came to their rescue.

Depression holed father and he developed heart ailment and passed away just four years after his son's missing. Alone and broken, the mother continued searching his son; went outside the state to locate him. The hope to see him alive was the only driving force. She visited most of the prisons but returned dejected.

Eighteen years down, the search has gradually stopped. Living in oblivion, the family has coped up gracefully with their grief. Poor old-mother and unmarried aged sisters have survived, and continue breathing on a feeble hope. Doing so, perhaps, remains a huge task in as dead a society they live in.

7

IS MEHDA KHAN ALIVE?

Your attention please! Ladies and gentlemen, you are welcome aboard Castle-

Air flight Number 420, that will be taking off at 1200 hrs BST (*Brazen-ia Standard Time*) in about 20 minutes from now, will be landing at "Brazenia air-strip". All the passengers are requested to fasten their seatbelts, keep their head straight and recite S-O-S (Songs of Sycophancy) as and when required during the flight.

Exactly 20 minutes later after this loaded announcement by air hostess, I stepped safely on the land of *Brazenia*. The clothy banner of 'changing colours' hanging above across the airport lounge entrance welcomed me. I had been here once, long back. So the vulnerable geography, whimsical climate, political gimmickry, economic jittery and of course, the cultural alchemy of *Brazenia* weren't at all alien to me. However, today I found myself in a preposterously changed ambience. I had come to meet *Mehda Khan* who was absconding since past few years and as per reports (unconfirmed) had re-surfaced lately on the scene. After hectic efforts, I was eventually able to have a dekko of him.

Today *Mehda Khan*, the epitome of habitants of *Brazenia*, is experiencing a 'release phenomenon'. He is no more the *Mehda Khan* of yesteryears who was complacent about almost everything, and mild in his opinions and judgments. Gone through a gross catalysis, he is jacked off. He is no more interested in listening to *Khabr-i-Zaina Kadal*. And why should he be, when the river flowing beneath *Zaina Kadal* has changed its colour abruptly from crimson to black. That's perhaps why he has alienated himself from the crowd passion of recent past, and has now taken a new kind of pep pill.

They say *Mehda Khan* has started volunteering the cause of human*ism*, activ*ism,* protection*ism* and *blah blah*, fast and furious. His *Dal Lake* is dying. His *Chinars* are gone. Mother language is failing. He is edgy about the "preservation". But, he is busy staging the shows of seminar syndrome, inviting anti-actuals to babble speeches on *Yemberzal* and *Masval*. And besides, to dabble in talks about *Balyaar, Madanwaar* and *Lolenaar.* 'Eggheads' feel pleased with his art of brown-nosing. Scientific speak is brushed off gullibly.

Not only this, rumours are rife that distressed *Mehda Khan* is inviting Arundhati Roy to inaugurate international conference on 'God of all things: from chameleons to crocodiles'. Special technical sessions about chameleon colours and crocodile tears will be conducted. The difference between Maoists and Militants will be touched over a tea-break. The gala event will be held at over-used State *Kabaab* International *Chai* Complex (SKICC) and the other dignitaries who are supposed to grace the occasion include *Sattara, Gaffara* and of course, the omnipresent *Akhbaarwalla.*

Mehda Khan is untiringly offering yeoman's service in organizing all esoteric jamborees for giving vent to the pent house of his feelings. Watching his chance, he is now saying and doing away everything he had forsaken temporarily. From Kashmiri pudding to Urdu dessert and from DD's puffing to Radio Kashmir's bluffing—he is now unhasped. He feels released, freed from shackles and is enjoying *Azadi Dil Ki.*

Apart from loitering around ravishing gardens, bewitching health resorts, junk food corners and glitter shops, *Mehda Khan* also emotively throngs shrines for the spiritual *Maasti.* No matter he is always out to cheat even God, but who says he is not God-fearing?!

The fact that *Mehda Khan* has fallen from grace does not strike his mind as he attributes his ideological volte-face to forced compromise and the changing taste of his compatriots whose youth has been benumbed by *B4U* shenanigans and Baywatch wannabees. And the older generation is busy in reviving the epicurean nostalgia.

The influences within and without have moulded *Mehda Khan* in a shocking way. Made to hang on to nostrums that seem quaint or dangerous, he has been actually desensitized regarding the very vital issues concerning him—a distant history, a tumultuous but misinterpreted present, a succession of disasters, a dreadful violence and crucial political failures. Trivialization has been pumped into his mind to an extent that he became a cabbage. *Mehda Khan* sans sense. Sans sensibility. Manipulation and mockery galore.

Finally, as I bid adieu to *Mehda Khan* it strikes my mind whether *Mehda Khan* is really alive or has he rechristened himself. The enigma was baffling.

Catching my return flight, I was in a wistful reverie. The moment plane flurried along the runway and pitched in the floating clouds, I was woken up by the morning crow of the cock. The beddy-byes were over but something was lingering within. Perhaps a bitter realization that the genome of *Mehda Khan* has undergone a drastic mutation, leading to an evolution of Frankstein Nation which **brazenly** refutes its history and **brazenly** refuses to reason, and is excelling only in giving alibis for every ill that has struck the land of *Brazenia*.

8

Covert Casualty to Conflict

Running down the thorny fields, she bleeds her feet. With misery, she looks around. She could only sight harvested fields with lifeless trees. The shady clouds in the sky didn't allow the sun to shine. She could hear nothing but the crackle of parched leaves she trampled upon with somberness. "Parisa, Parisa", she yelled impulsively for her sweet little daughter whom she had lost somewhere.

Before she could really gather herself, suddenly her husband woke her up. "Thank Heavens, I was just dreaming", she said to him, taking a deep icy breath. Soon she moved towards the bedroom of Parisa. Opening the door unhurriedly, she found Parisa in a deep sleep. She sat beside her bed and didn't sleep for rest of the night.

The coming dawn was quite unusual for Parisa. When she got up, she found mom caressing her.

"My darling, stay back with me today. Don't go anywhere", she told while holding her.

Mom seemed edgy and down in the dumps. That day she prepared breakfast half-heartedly. Something she couldn't express was making her glum and sad.

As the overcast sky started a bit gleaming, Parisa was in to her own things. "Mom, I am going to market with Baba. Bolt the door, bye", Parisa shouted from the main gate. Before cheerless Mom could come out of the kitchen to stop her, frolic Parisa had already left alongwith her *Baba*. She anxiously rang up the cell phone of her husband just to find it switched off.

It was lunch time. She had prepared Parisa's favourite food. She preferred to wait till she returns. It took a bit long for Parisa to be back.

Ding Dong! The door-bell buzzed. She hastily rushed to open the door only to see a few of her neighbours, wearing a vague look. "What happened? Tell me", she asked them timidly. "Nothing, don't worry. Parisa just fainted on the main road. She has been taken to the hospital", one of them said discreetly.

She was taken aback. Got stunned but mustered courage to ask, "Please tell me the truth". After a brief awkward pause, a voice came, "Actually . . . . she was hit by a speeding security vehicle while she was crossing the road . . . ." On hearing this, she was iced over with a shocker, speechless and staggered.

The grey afternoon had arrived. Sun had failed to come out with complete refulgence. Day was bloated with precarious shadows. Parisa's naive smile wasn't everlasting. Another innocent had felt prey to the speeding vehicle of security forces. She had not fallen to bullet or bomb shell. The obvious crossfire of conflict hadn't consumed her. Her fate was not 'newsworthy' to be covered by NDTV or AajTak, except a small news agency report picked up by some newspapers . . . 'Girl killed in road crash in Kashmir. An enraged mob torched two army vehicles in Jammu and Kashmir after an army truck in a convoy ran over a girl . . . .' *(ANI, 8 Sept., 2009)*

Parisa was battling in hospital. Her mother was not allowed to see her. She was put on ventilator in an Intensive Care Unit (ICU). Breathing artificially with no gesture or life on her face, she had gone in to coma.

Parisa's shattered parents would only gaze her expressionless face and morbid eyes through a small glass opening of ICU door. They were restless and fidgety. Doctors had not given them any assurance. Parisa was still in a very serious condition.

While solacing them, relatives and acquaintances dropped in and talked about the mishaps that have been occurring because of the over-speeding by unregistered security vehicles in the State. Some talked about the statistics which revealed that now road-accidents claim more lives than armed conflict in the State. Everyone seemed to imply that if law gives a particular imprisonment for hitting someone on road for civil drivers, why the same could not be applied for non-civil drivers as well. The casual discussions and conversations went on as visitors arrived and departed.

Meanwhile, Parisa, the girl whom her mother kissed often, and the child whom her father admired immensely, looked unfathomably dead to the world though something was little by little corroding her inwardly.

9

Down the Lake

The wrinkled face was parched and frail like a fallen Chinar leaf in autumn, which once looked green and glorious. Behind the old visage, there was more of him to see. Struggling between past and future, verve and sloth, triumphs and letdowns, warmth and seclusion—he was coldly looking at the sophisticated and expensive Finnish machines procured to speed-up Dal Lake's restoration measures.

This old man was sitting near the railing on the banks of Dal Lake watching the slough and silt that was being lifted from the Lake.

He recollected the days of his childhood when he alongwith his friends used to quench his thirst with the shimmering sweet waters of Dal Lake. The images of nostalgia tossed around. Like an antique montage in black and white, the screen of history flashed his every memory associated with Dal Lake.

Looking back, he saw himself playing football in *Malkhah* graveyard for hours together, and then rushing to *Naidyar Yarbal* to slake their thirst with the cool, refreshing and flowing pure water of the Dal. At times, his whole group of friends swam into the water to revitalize themselves.

The old man remembered how once one of his friends got his cycle for cleansing at *Yarbal* and he was not allowed to do so by a local resident, giving the reason that the water was used for cooking purposes by many families.

The unique taste of *Masala Roti* he used to have beneath the shade of jade trees on *Soth*, the bridle path passing through the middle of the Dal Lake connecting Nishat and Rainawari, remained persisting. The cold breeze that tenderly moved the crystal clear waters of the Lake was embedded with the aroma of versatile lotuses.

As the Lake was bottomless near *Soth*, he and his friends always feared swimming there. Watching small yachts being drawn by oars and gently passing under the arched seven viaducts of *Soth*, they always craved to go in swimming in the deep central waters of the Lake. They incessantly desired to spend a few days in the straggling row of majestic-looking *Doongas* that flanked the Lake at various points and were rented by people to roam around the Lake for several days.

In his youth, Dal Lake was his true companion. He relished veritable solace on its banks. Looking far to the other end of Lake, he used to weave his future plans. It was his usual to prepare for his exams on the shores of Lake. Whenever he was depressed, he went to the Lake and poured his heart out. Dal always listened calmly and transpired its tranquility to him.

Sometime later he got married. He decided to holiday in the Lake alongwith his family and a small group of friends. They hired a *Donga* for one week and also arranged a *Waza* who would accompany them on *Donga* and prepare food for them during the expedition.

The reminiscences of the matchless trip were sharply ingrained in his mind. He mused over the setting of their voyage from *Naidyar Yarbal*. For him and his friends, it was like dream coming true. The sparkling and soft waters helped the stately progress of *Doonga* down the Lake. They were welcomed by the breezy milieu while sailing down the watercourse through the interiors of Rainawari. The banks of waterway were spotless. Only at few places, they could see some temporary hutments and some planted vegetables.

Within the blissful vibes, the immaculate waters of the Lake were reflecting the vivid image of splendid dome of *Hazratbal* Shrine, where they stopped for the night. They watched scores of people performing their ablution with the fresh waters of the Lake. Interestingly, their waza also had used the Lake water for cooking during the whole journey.

While travelling towards *Nishat* garden, they noticed water gushing out from the bottom of the Lake at numerous locations. During night, they saw moonlight piercing through the six meter deep clear waters of the Lake and getting reflected after striking its bottom. With a bit of edginess, they went for a dip in the deep waters of the Lake, and thus conquered their fears.

Harking back, the old man remembered that the banks of the Lake had no fencing around as Nature by its own course had fenced it with the Zabarwan hills on one side and the Hari-parbat on the other. Nature had swathed the glistening waterbody with its own aura.

However today, he is stunned, the crinkled moist eyes, the crooked forehead. He fails to think of Dal Lake as "a beautiful imagination or a romantic poetry on the surface of clean water shadowed with the groves of Chinar" by visitors.

Ironically, Dal Lake has become a cesspool. A stinking abyss. A nearing gutter. The shrinking pit that has obnoxious and murky stories buried in it. The stories of Corruption; Official Fraud; Public Apathy; and General Malice.

For the old man, the cesspit, now left as Dal, depicts a broader meaning: it is a manifestation of collective mind. The degeneration is not just ecological.

He takes small steps, away from the Lake, as if a strong wind could, at any time, whisk him up into the clouds. He leaves no footprints.

10

Heroes Beyond Rhetoric

"Sir, will we be back in Srinagar by 4:30 evening"? asked the Sumo driver. "Hopefully, yes. But why are you asking so?" replied one among the group of passengers. "Sir, actually I have promised my fiancé to see her at 5:30. We are getting married soon", the driver said. He was probably worried because of the road condition and rainy forecast while driving towards frontier area.

That day the dawn was overcast and sun had not shown its face fairly. "Wake up my dear, you had told me yesterday to awaken you early", while caressing his hair, mother told him. "Yes, today I am going to a far-off place with my passengers", he replied while rubbing his eyes. After getting ready, he said to his mother, "I am going Mom. I may come late". Half-heartedly his mother saw him off and said, "I will be worried, drive carefully".

The young man had recently got engaged and he had fixed a date with his fiancé in the evening of that very day. Turning nights into days, he was always on move, looking for opportunities to earn more. Besides earning the livelihood for his parents, he was putting all his blood and sweat to sum up extra money for his marriage. He was true to life. He had no romantic vision to pursue. He just had a reliable mission. A realistic goal—To be the support of his family and earn for their happiness. Honestly and gracefully.

It was April 20, 2004. He rushed to the place from where he had to fetch a team of passengers who had hired his vehicle to monitor the first phase of elections in Northern Kashmir. Since some of the persons who had to accompany the group did not turn up because of certain reasons, a seat got vacant after the designated individuals boarded the vehicle. Seeing this, one of the lady members of the team displayed her interest in accompanying the team and boarded the vehicle. The voyage started. The driver might have been skeptical but was brave enough to accompany the team on a risky assignment because he was simply clear about doing his job.

All along the way, he was thinking of shaping his humble dreams into hardcore realities. The clouds had begun to veil the place that he was cruising through. After driving out of the village near the *Line of Control* (LoC), where the team was on a monitoring exercise, he had no idea that he was literally holding the steering of life of everyone in his vehicle, including himself. He was moving towards the next destination. The ultimate one. The destination was getting closer. So was death.

'Bang!' A sudden thud. His vehicle was ripped off. Startling darkness draped everything around.

41

Dense shady smoke was the only shroud. It was a landmine blast. His vehicle had detonated an explosive device. Ghulam Nabi Sheikh, the unsung hero, was blown up by the bomb not targeted either for him or anyone else on board.

Cruelly, the destiny had played its role by offering a vacant seat in the vehicle to a courageous human rights activist who also lost her life in this gruesome incident. She, as reported, was helping a local human rights group prepare an account of its election monitoring activity.

Ghulam Nabi may have faded into oblivion but his mention cannot be rendered obscure. He symbolizes a common Kashmiri whose sacrifice and service is usually trapped and stamped out under the huge rhetorical discourse. He never becomes a cover story. His story remains unaccounted and unreported.

Perhaps, a man in a street, a face in a crowd, a commoner in Kashmir has no glorification added to his daily struggle. He lives and dies unknown and un-mourned. His blood offers no inspiration to a generation that is fast and gets easily carried away. The shades of reality, in an original form, never get unraveled before them. They don't even strive to discover them because the rhetoric is so compelling to them.

In Kashmir, people lost lots of men without actually knowing who they have lost. This is very tragic and disgraceful as well. The life and death of Ghulam Nabi and his ilk, has always failed to inscribe its significance on the pages of their ever-distorted history. And that remains the reason of the unending chaos surrounding Kashmir.

11

'WE ARE ALL POLITICS'

"I witnessed such a windstorm for the first time", my friend said while we were travelling home. As roads were deserted and an eerie silence was breaking down with blowing winds, we were just skeptical about reaching home safely. 'Trin-Trin', her cell phone buzzed. "Don't attend any more calls. The blustery weather is getting creepy", I said grabbing her cellphone. I actually knew that if she picks up the phone, I will be left alone to my frightful thoughts. I was simply scared stiff about the strong winds tossing against the moving car. Her phone buzzed again. "Let me see, it may be something important", she said while taking her cellphone back. "It is an unknown number to me", she murmured and received the call.

Although I wasn't keenly listening to her conversation over phone, but I could gather that she was being invited for some meeting. As I dropped her, she told me that it was a call from a known politician. "Will you go for the meet?" I asked curiously.

Stepping out from the car, she gave a sarcastic smile across the window pane and said, "Of course I will! After all, we all are politics".

Wind was wafting, harsh and hard. Dust was swirling all around. The hum of wind was getting gusty. Cloudy skies were putting across a strange message. Somehow, I reached home.

The next day whirlwind had settled. The talk of damages was making rounds everywhere. Weather man's forecast was vindicated. The day passed calmly.

In the evening, around 10 O'clock, the sudden bang horrified me. Is it the tempest again? No! Lifting the curtain, I peeped through the window and saw a blaze of fire-crackers bursting in my locality. It was complemented with shouts and hoots. The Cricket Asia Cup 2012 final had just concluded. Pakistan had won the trophy. I wasn't amazed. It wasn't a storm of any kind. Just a few days ago, when one of the cabinet ministers had visited our area, the din of fire-crackers had produced the similar scene.

As the clamor settled and night wrapped up the ambience in darkness, I recalled my friend's words the other day. I tried to grasp what actually she wanted to convey.

We are all politics. From our domestic affairs to anything around, the politics is embedded in us. We play politics every day, every moment. The politics floats up from our homes and sneaks into our social circles and workplaces. It breaks the surface and slithers into every aspect. Even politics slips in Politics. In bigger subjects. In biggest matters.

Of course, no person can keep away from the sirens of politics. It's impossible to stuff the politics altogether. To quote the French critic, Max Adereth, "the inescapable moral is that even if we ignore politics, politics will not ignore us". There is, no doubt, the archetypal allergy of the contemplating mind to the ugly and abrasive business of politics. Politics here, politics there. There is certainly something in this brutal business which compels a falsification of factuality. No sensitive soul may survive in such a kind of moral squalor without paying a heavy price. The erosion in the end makes an otherwise fertile mind an impostor in retreat, before the assaults of reality. And that happens to be the fate of all of us, in this part of the world.

Some thinkers believe that eventually politics will die, but everything will be politics. That's to say, politics will creep in our lives. And it has already. All our doings stand politicized.

From offering prayers to paying condolences to playing in official chairs, nothing seems devoid of politics. And it can't be otherwise now. Politics— whether in common dusty street or in an ostentatious cosy office—has become a lifeline for small-minded people like us.

Irony, nonetheless, remains that while being 'political' in most spheres of our life, we fail to comprehend that we are essentially playing politics with ourselves. We stand politicized. It is virtually turning us hypocrite. The 'dual-people' lacking conviction, right or wrong.

The night outside was slowly receding into the recesses of oblivion, mutely closing the turbulent chapter of day gone-by. It will happen over and again. The cycle will not break. Of course, not till the stormy wind breaks the deceptive stillness and delivers a tough point.

12

RELOCATING LOSS

"Please be careful with her"! With curiosity and distress, he said to the nurse who was about to put venous catheter on his daughter's hand. The newborn baby was referred to children's hospital for some breathing problem, wherein she was admitted for intravenous medication. The ward had several warmers where tiny tender souls were lying in bed rows. Few of them had oxygen masks and some had intravenous fluids dripped to them. Due to scarcity of staff, the anxious parents were themselves constantly checking the oxygen masks and the intravenous lines given to their infants.

No sooner the ward nurse pricked the supple little hand of his daughter, he fled the scene. He couldn't tolerate the sight of blood oozing out from her baby's hand while the catheter was put in place. "It is done", said the nurse while calling him and added, "Get the prescribed injections till I direct dextrose to her". With dismay, he inquired, "How much would it cost?"

Sensing his helplessness, the nurse replied, "You go to the drug store of the hospital. You will get it free". On hearing this, he regained some confidence and rushed to the hospital drug store.

"Here I am", he said while handing over two injection vials to the nurse, who had already started intravenous fluid through micro dropper. Now he was hopeful that his daughter will recover because of the medication. He was watching eagerly while the nurse was gradually emptying the contents of the syringe into the bloodstream of his daughter. He was glad to learn from the nurse that his daughter was not critical now, and if the treatment had to continue, he should get the medicines from the hospital drug store.

"Hey, you are yet sitting here! You told me that you are going to peg the cattle in the hutch after listening to the news". Suddenly he gathered himself and found an old radio near him in a shanty room having a small light lit in a corner, and his fuming wife standing at the door. He was swirled into the flashback of the tragedy he had gone through after listening to the news about spurious drugs in hospitals of Kashmir.

A few months ago, his wife had delivered a baby girl who was admitted in Children's Hospital for some breathing distress though her condition was not critical. As a poor father, he was not in a position to buy the medicines and got the same from the hospital drug store supplies. To the worst of his luck, the treatment proved ineffective. The condition of sweet little angel was getting worse. Eventually, the innocent soul took the wings and left for heavenly abode.

He had lost his trust in doctors. But today, he was realizing that the tool of a treating physician was rendered worthless by spurious elements. The one that have acted as a slow poison that was being steadily injected into his daughter's blood. He now understood that his daughter was not struggling against any disease but was fighting deadly injections that were subtly invading her all organ systems.

The distressed man left the room without a word. The bereaved wife just looked on with surprise. Done with his cattle, he went to a nearby shop just to deflect his mind from painful memory and joined the people who were idling there. "Tomorrow, again a *Hartal*!" said one of the persons who was rummaging the pages of a local newspaper. The shutdown call was given to protest against spurious drug scam. It was to be a maiden apolitical strike in Kashmir to express the resentment peacefully. Hearing about it, the distraught father regained a faint confidence, a kind of slight poise that thousands of people will empathize with him and share his concern over the precious loss.

The daily reports of spurious drug scam did not appear convincing to him. He was doubtful about the ways authorities were responding to such serious issue. His cute baby had been got snatched because of this menace and many more too had faced its wrath. And the long term repercussions on those who were continuously consuming the spurious drugs were alarming. For him, it was a slow and sure genocide. By whom—the question was a horrifying riddle for him and his ilk.

Next morning, he woke up, had his tea and started towards an adjoining town through the green meadows. The firmly standing trees and green blossom around infused resilience in him. He felt it was *his day* today. The day to register his resentment, his concern.

On reaching the town, he discovered he was alone. In the din of crowd and ceaseless honking, he was lost in a blank isolation. He could situate only moving faces and running vehicles. He had to relocate his loss, his sorrow, his perception. But, the repositioning was difficult and dire. For him and his ilk.

"Conflict within and without has done its job", he murmured and walked amidst the strange faces and faded out somewhere in the smog and dust of the town.

CHARACTERS

13

OBLIVION SALVAGES

In the dead of dreaded night, she suspiciously moved out of her old house. Her feet were shaky and her body was shivering. With fright on her face, she was concealing something beneath her *Pheran*. Once she was sure that she is not being spotted by anyone, she made her way towards deserted fields. Terrified by the voice of barking dogs, she hurriedly took out something from her *Pheran* and started burying it in the soil. Nervously she covered every bit of it with bits of grass and litter around, and fled the place.

Back home, her son saw her coming and angrily asked, "Where were you? Isn't it surprising that you left *Masooma* alone in her room?" The fearful mother stammered and said, "Nothing, I was just . . . ." Without completing, she rushed to her daughters' room. The son took it casually and went to sleep.

Next morning, he woke up late, as his mother had not given a wakeup knock at his door. Anxiously, he moved out from his bed and started looking for her.

He went to *Masooma's* room who gave her brother an unusual smile. He was somewhat upset to see the strange unease and disquiet at his home. He again spotted his mother entering the house. No sooner she stepped in, he said to her, "Why are you behaving so oddly, and why are your hands soiled?" The panicky mother tried to clean her hands on her back while saying, "I am just tired".

Few days passed but the gloom and dismay at his home persisted. Meanwhile, *Masooma* developed some fever. "Mother, let us take her to the doctor", said the son. "It is a simple fever, she will be alright soon", mother replied coldly. Her weird behavior annoyed him. He got up furiously, banged the door, and left his home. His apprehensions that his mother was concealing something began getting strong.

Sun was dipping behind the mountains and the darkness was at hand. All of a sudden, mother heard some people rushing towards the fields and shouting, "What is it, why are dogs barking?" Unnerved, she hurried to the spot. She saw her son and other people at a place emanating stench. Without caring for the people around, the son said to his mother, "I saw you visiting this place several times, can you . . . .". "Hey! here is something under this soil", one person interrupted, pointing his finger towards the spot. He covered up his face and started digging up. "What the hell is this?" he cried, as everybody got stunned. A small piece of decomposed flesh, a body of a newborn was unearthed. The mother broke down and fell in a faint. Her son, who was at a loss to understand anything, comforted the mother till she regained conscious.

Before anybody could ask her anything, she said to her son, "*Masooma* gave birth to this dead child, and I secretly buried him here". He was stunned and speechless. He lifted the stinky body of newborn and wrapped it in a small cloth. Everybody around was taken aback as everyone knew that his sister was not married. "This is a heinous act, we should inform police", said one of the elderly persons in a group.

Next day, a police squad and team of doctors rushed to their home. A huge crowd, drawing people from all over the village of *Arizaal,* was seen sympathizing with the brother and the mother of the victim. The police head took brother and mother in isolation for questioning. "I know it is a moment of grief for you, but I need to do my duty. Was she having any relation . . . ." Before the man in uniform would complete, the brother held his hand and led him and the doctors to *Masooma's* room. They saw a frail figure huddled around by women. The brother asked the women to leave the room as police and medical staff had to question *Masooma.*

A young girl in her early twenties was lying motionless on the bed. She only smiled at everyone. Before anyone could say anything, the brother uttered with difficulty, "She is my younger sister . . . . Since her birth, I and my mother have been taking care of her", taking a heavy sigh he slowly sat beside her and added in a choked voice, "she smiles at everyone as she does not know what has happened to her . . . . she is physically challenged and mentally retarded". On hearing this, all took a step back. It was difficult for them to imagine such a sexual assault been inflicted on a one who has a deranged mind and a diseased body, and who is not knowing who she is. Her spastic limbs and drooling mouth was pulling the pathetic attention towards her.

Both *Masooma* and her exhumed baby were shifted to the block hospital. As *Masooma* could not utter a word about what had happened with her and who was behind the gruesome crime, it was decided to take the newborn for postmortem. The postmortem team conducted autopsy on a tiny piece of flesh and send the samples for forensic tests.

Masooma did not know what being a mother means. She did not even know what being a woman means. A criminal sick mind in her part of world, which she did not know is called Kashmir, had behaved worse than an animal with her.

Seems okay that she is oblivious of everything and remains so always. Her limbo is her salvation.

14

ALIEN AGONY

Thud. Thud. It was an unusual knock. She curiously rushed to open the door. It was her father. He wore an unusual look, his eyes grim and face long. Without uttering anything, he kissed her forehead and went inside. He was in a dilemma. His friend had proposed a boy, settled abroad, for the marriage of his daughter.

It was a middle class family putting up in one of the congested areas of downtown. He was reluctant to think over this offer as his daughter had never even ventured out of home city. It was only after lot of contemplation and conversation that his wife convinced him to consider this proposal. As a routine, daughter submitted to her parents will. The father used some sources to enquire about the boy and his family. Apparently everything seemed good. As such, father had no reason but to accept the proposal.

The prospective groom was informed about this. He too gave his consent. Moreover, he had assured his parents that he was not interested in marrying anyone except the girl belonging to his homeland. The boy managed to acquire one months' leave from his workplace. He informed his parents to fix the marriage date during the same period. As time was less, the marriage was held in a simple way.

Sometime after marriage, the boy returned back to his place of work promising to send a family visa for his wife within a fortnight. He kept his word and sent a visa and air ticket for his wife.

Back home, the parents of the girl were packing things for her. From small packets of Kashmiri rice to all cooking spices, her mother stuffed almost everything in her luggage. Her father decided to accompany her to Delhi wherefrom she had to board international flight.

Endless roads, Manhattan buildings and lush motor cars: the world she had seen on small screen, was beckoning her. She was inquisitive to see this all. In fact, the new world meant many different things for her. A wonderful experience which touches deepest emotions. A quite understanding, mutual confidence, sharing and forgiving. A loyalty through good and bad times. The world that settles for less than perfection and makes allowances for human weaknesses. Harbours contentment with the present, hope for the future and no brooding over the past. The day-in and day-out chronicle of problems, compromises, disappointments amidst small achievements and little joys. Above all, the new world made up for the many things the girl had missed: maybe an innocent smile; a selfless gesture; the sincerity of purpose; and the significance of honesty in everything.

Wishing her good luck, father saw her off with tearful eyes. But an unknown fear and distress veiled his smile. He wasn't that happy.

Plane took off. She was flying for the first time. She was not alone, but carried along her dreams as well. She was all set to devote her everything to husband.

After a long travel, she reached the destination safely and was pleased to see her husband waiting for her at the airport. Not knowing what to speak, surprised and confused, she was peeping through the window pane of the radio cab while moving towards her new home. She was amazed to see her husband having cooked some food for her. They sat together and had the first dinner abroad.

What she had been taught by her parents, she began to practice. She gradually took the responsibility of household. One afternoon, just a few months later, while busy with her chores, she received a call from her husband saying he would come late tonight. She waited for her on dinner but he turned up very late in night. She didn't express her annoyance but felt it badly. This was the first time she sensed an emotional hurt.

As days passed, his late coming became a norm. She felt that he was getting indifferent towards her. Nonetheless, she consoled herself by attributing his nonchalance to probably mounting pre-occupation at his workplace.

Again, some months later she came to know that she was blessed with the most precious gift of mankind. She was in a family way. She excitedly informed her husband about it. But there was a huge shock stored in his reply—"It is the time for making our future, and I don't want more responsibilities right now. We will abort it before it's too late." It cost her mental peace and solace for resisting not to end her pregnancy. The ordeal was agonizing. Now life and love connoted an obscurely tough battle for her. It brought to fore everything that she had never imagined. She discovered herself and the world, and then forgot only to discover them again and again. The process of waking never slipped back, and never was she free of herself. Like flowing up and down from a trance, she lodged herself in an eerily familiar life already well under way. She was both observer and observable, an object of her own excruciating awareness.

It was during the last trimester of her pregnancy when a pretty young lady of the foreign land approached her alongwith two kids and revealed that she is wedded to her husband and the kids belong to him. This was the last nail in the coffin. She had nothing to say. She informed her parents. They were shattered.

The moment her husband came to know that nothing is now hidden from her and her family, he brutally thrashed her out of his home.

In an alien country, she came on road. She had no place to go. She had nothing to survive on. Some charity organizations helped her to deliver her baby in a hospital.

Along with her newborn child, she ultimately landed on the unfamiliar streets to beg and gather some money to buy a return ticket to her home.

The grief-stricken parents kept waiting for her arrival.

15

OUR ALI BABA

As kids all of us must have felt fascinated and bemused on hearing the most famous and celebrated story of Arabian Nights *Ali Baba and Forty Thieves*. One of the fictional characters based in Ancient Arabia, Ali Baba, was a poor woodcutter who happened to overhear a group of thieves, forty in all, visiting their treasure store in the forest where he is cutting wood. The thieves' treasure is in a cave, the mouth of which is sealed by magic—it opens on the words *Open Sesame*. When the thieves are gone, Ali Baba enters the cave himself, and takes some of the treasure home.

These days so many names are linked to "Ali Baba". That's why we hear "Ali Baba" yellings associated to the names of all the presumably 'prominent' people. *Ala* Saddam Hussain: he was a *big Ali Baba*. George Bush: he was a *bigger Ali Baba*. Nonetheless, Saddam and Bush are only the tip of the Ali Baba iceberg. The label can apply to a multitude of other persons or typified characters of certain nations.

In fact, there's another aspect to the *Ali Baba labeling* phenomenon. The name Ali Baba has become somewhat of a misnomer. Ali Baba was an indigent man who became rich unexpectedly by stealing from the treasure of notorious thieves. His most notable traits were an incredible credulity and a kind of bigoted unawareness to looming danger.

So, even though he surely wasn't the villain in the story, and certainly not the cunning, his name has become synonymous with sham and sting nowadays. It isn't that astonishing. Ali Baba was poor. However, he wasn't completely upright. He laid his hands on all that was ill-gotten.

Well, those were bygone days. Things have changed and so have the thinkings. If, at all, we could have the remake of this story today, we would see Ali Baba nourishing the evil men, *the Forty Thieves*, to use them someday for fulfilling his ulterior motives. Or, may be Ali Baba would himself hide in one of the oil pots to express his sympathy with the evil doers! Our mutated Ali Baba would not stop there, but would multiply his forty men to forty thousand and may be more.

Coming to Kashmir, Ali Baba is enormously conspicuous and very much metaphorical. It would be interesting to see *Ali Baba* in a new *avatar*, in more than *Forty Crafty Roles*, from *Nayak to Khal Nayak*. The legendary Ali Baba would not be alone but his clones and dummies would dot every nook and corner.

In fact, we would see Ali Babas' galore. Our streets, mohallas, offices, educational institutions and centres, banks and business establishments would thrive on existence of Ali Baba(s). Not strange, that most of our politicians would have already graduated as *supertime-Ali Babas,'* and mind you, that would initiate debate as to whether we should have any government policy for code of conduct for Ali Baba, his behavior, actions and dealings with common people, and also his dress code.

The Ali Baba of yore would be anything but a naiveté in life. He would require a hardened, brutal and unscrupulous mindset with a soft, gentle and elitist demeanor. He would require being adept at twisting and distorting that which is real, alive and important to replace the same by gimmicks, slogans, muck-racking and subtle-slander.

Ah! He would be techno-savvy and media-savvy too. A laptop, palmtop, and whatever would be tucked unto him and he would talk in air about the Net, the Bluetooth, Facebook *et al*. He would be there to hog the limelight wherever there would be the glitz and the glam. The paparazzi would adore him for all the eccentricities.

The Ali Baba (metamorphosed) would go lock, stock and barrel for gaining riches, fame and name. The *raison detre* of Ali Baba would be *moolah*—at all costs. Ethics, principles and steadfastness would be his *bete noire*. He would occupy high positions through fawning and flattery. And then, dabble in all kinds of fraud, sleaze and manipulation to justify his occupation.

The Ali Baba of present-day would make it a point to get his progeny settled anywhere he finds a chance to slay someone else's merit and stake. Trampling down all rules and regulations, he would knock over and mould ways to see his kith and kin having a smooth sailing in life. Be it politics, bureaucracy or any other establishment, he would lay the plush *foundation* for his mediocre *Gen Next.*

The contemporary Ali Baba would steal or snatch, and even beg or borrow to flaunt his false prestige in a society. Be it marriage ceremony, religious pilgrimage, *rasm-e-chahrum* or any other social gathering, he would do all things to keep up his phony and bogus social stature.

The reality remains that existing Ali Baba is a unique creature who rocks his colors every now and then to fit in any situation gratifying to him. He swaps and swoops his outfit over and over again. He is a shallow person. Even as ghosts are flabbergasted to see him changing roles, the people surround and admire him. He is applauded for his knack of passing on charade as chivalry. The facade he puts up is rarely exposed . . .

I am here
on this street corner.
I am calling out
you there.
The haze of shouts
blurs my entreaty.
The lamp on the pole
blinkers your vision.
The loneliness

smothers my being.
The crowds
surround you in vain.
Roads are blocked
for me.
Pathways of deceit
welcome you.
Angels chase me.
Ghosts stare you.
I am bound to
stand and wait.
You are enticed to
move and go.
I am colourless
I am happy.
You became a chameleon,
you are sadly inhuman.

Glorified for every wrong, he is bound to get huge social acclaim. And, why not?! His blinkered vision is as dogmatic as the society he lives in. A place where sanity is scorned, criticism is shown contempt, and rectitude is ridiculed, Ali Baba is assured to have a field day. He will keep crawling up the ladder of "success". No surprises!!

16

MR. KNOW ALL

Pessimist; cynic; wise-crack; pedantic; pugnacious—all packed into one. Let's call him 'XLR'—no connotations, mind you! And you may replace that by ALR, BLR etc., of course, with the exception of *SLR*. For it may hurt him as also others who drink, eat, sleep and ease-out in the shade of *SLR's*.

Well, what is so special about this XLR that prompted me to pen down these words? Beginning with physical features, XLR has a round face, medium height and built, grey hair (occasionally dyed), keen sight and hearing, even though his age demands him to be rather senile. XLR's face presents an academic look with clear signs of having been a 'struggling person', a fighter during his youth.

XLR's demeanor is marked by his grumbling and groaning all the time. Not that he hasn't achieved anything, but over a period of time he has developed 'the trait of being a man'. He thinks, but in a perverted manner; talks, but in a contemptuous way; observes, but only the negative aspect of things; and—works, only to show his indispensability. XLR has the nagging habit of projecting himself as a Mr. Know-All. If only it could be so however!

XLR is not a jovial personality but loves to dish out double meaning statements, sugar coated abuses and deprecating remarks in presence of his colleagues. For he thinks that he is the most grandiloquent person around his workplace. Lastly, XLR is a bore of first rate, and he will never leave you unless he has narrated half a dozen anecdotes with the use of refined intermittent invectives that serve as incipient and preservatives in a tale full of concoctions, false conclusions and pejorative inferences about people, places and men of reckoning. XLR likes to talk about his version of *tantra, mantra* and worn out *parampara* only to keep his talking *yantra* (mouth) in good shape.

Who says XLR has no high contacts. He brags of being a so-called CBC (Cosmopolitan By Chance) because having migrated from his native place, he resides on the other side of Pir-Panjal pass, has progeny seeking education beyond *Vindhyas* on one side and *Hindukush* on the other. Thanks to XLR's sympathizers in the Saffron brigade, quotas within quotas and subcategories within categories have been arranged for his off springs. And why not, the children of XLR are not only born but have been borne to rule all the time, everywhere. The meek, submissive and humble XLR of yesteryears has gone beyond all limits to show his Nietzscheian prowess. A bang-up job, he has full time at his native place and to rob the coffers of State in the name of 'relief', he moves to the other side of the tunnel every now and then.

Politically his brain is a live wire of 'fascism' *ala* Punit Issar of *Hindustani* fame. Undoubtedly, given a chance XLR will never budge an inch to practice the ideals of *Chengaiz Khan* and *Halaku* to achieve his utopian ideal—a virtual heaven much like the *Jannat-of-Shadaad,* with some modern additions such as combatant security bandobast.

To boot, XLR has time and again given the proof of being a first-hand patriot which many a time borders upon foolhardiness, much like the Danny Dengzongpa showing his shenanigans in *Ajnabi.* Of late, his progeny has started cooking "creative narratives" to sell their tale of prejudice, and project themselves as "only victims". And then, there are so many takers for victimhood stories by non-residents of this place!

Hey, hold it, hold it! Who is this XLR, by the way? Well, don't panic. This is not fantasy and neither am I talking about any garbage bag. Actually, XLR is you know who. He can be anybody's erstwhile neighbour or a boyhood chum or else the much revered pedagogue—all of whom managed that *Great Escape* from the 'disputed territory' which they think is worse than an *Alkatrass* Prison. No matter XLR keeps on shuttling to see the plight of its inmates and also to collect his monthly packet. He has somehow been successful to turn this *Alkatrass* into a virtual Dubai for himself.

XLR is not a new man. He may have changed his habits partially to suit the moods, tantrums and histrionics of his sugar daddies and godfathers in polity, bureaucracy and power corridors, however it goes without saying that XLR was and is an, opportunist to the hilt, a chameleon that has put to shame all and sundry of his community. He knows no morals, ethics or principles. He wants to excel everywhere all the time, come what the cost. Perhaps that is why he is called "Exceller" (XLR).

That's the bottom line!

17

WINTER'S WOES

These long dark, cold nights and dry chilly days. Long queues around and a mad rush for anything available. As we grope in the dark, confused as ever, we brace ourselves up to welcome him with unease, discomfort and melancholy.

An anathema to the poor and sick, but portending a gala time for elite. As he starts his sojourn, come miseries galore. Spiraling prices, power cuts, frozen taps, scarce commodities and chaotic roads. Problems and problems all the way, for those who don't forget the New Year in their dreams. No, they don't ever! Actually, they fail to remember it.

A voice says, "Hey, Hello! Happy New Year. I am from the *Rangeen* Palace. We are having a nice dinner party, and an exclusively, for couples ball dance tonight. Happy New Year to you too . . . ." The phone snapped.

Inside a departmental store, he saw guys and gals buying New Year cards, souvenirs, talking hearts, and all that which matters to the love sick and love-stupid. Some making hush-hush buzz calls, giggling, smiling, and oblivious of their future and of him. One among them hissing . . . . "Hello! *Hello-Farmayish!* Can you play *Kuch Kuch Hota Hai?"*

Screeching to an abrupt halt, he sees a black Scorpio vehicle, the occupants in tight jeans, spotting Raybans. With contemptuous eyes, they, the neo—riche, scan the Sunday market, where teeming crowds look for cheaper clothes to save themselves from the frozen turbulence. *"Yaar, yeh second—hand maal hai!* (Friends, It's a second-hand stuff).Let's go to the Wearhouse", they fret.

He boards a bus, plying through the bad narrow roads of Srinagar, as if traversing the clogged arteries of its bruised heart. The bus was overflowing with passengers, jostling, sneering, arguing, and hoping that this winter gets dry for otherwise they will be out of work. It is a prayer that is poison to the ears of eco-freaks, for they want us to see mountains yelling with snow and rivers barking with water. After all, *'Power Ka Sawaal hai!'* (It is the matter of Power).

As he went down the bus, a hundred people crossing the road, accompanying the coffin to graveyard, their faces sullen and wry, he asked, "Who was he?" "He was an oldie, suffering from asthma. Winter took toll of him" . . . . Yet another quipped—*"Wakht Aosus Wotmut"* (His time was up).

In a daily paper, he read a dozen obits about *Rasm-e-Chahrum.* Unnerved, disturbed and panicky, he yearned for a place where he could hide in sorry. He managed a place in the cozy *Hammam* of a mosque, where young and old were gossiping, talking all but Allah. Exasperated, he left straight for the airport. Caught in crossfire and jammed roads, he however missed the flight and returned back with a heavy heart.

He is waiting for the flight, fervently longing to leave, for his presence here except to a minuscule-elite, is agonizing. He sighs, "I wish never to visit this place ever again!"

Yes, he is Winter of Kashmir. Actually, there is always a mystical sense of reality captured by the shock and bewilderment associated with his arrival. Everything slows in stillness but a strange yell remains shrieking in the backdrop. We seem trapped in a world of anger, rage, harshness, misery and we see only red through our eyes. Rarely any one seems to see when we are going through this frozen time, or understand why.

Epilogue-The common masses of Kashmir are hemmed in the same paradox of aching pain. Everything is a lie for them. Vanishing hopes and broken promises smother their being. Even as they put up a façade of *usual* living, they are lost in a silent rant and rave, a simmering discontent.

Affairs here are always in a bedlam. There is an absolute anarchy, especially on administrative front. Every winter we are witness to things that are hallmark of Kashmir; its *USP* so to say. The Snowfall. Snapped Electricity. Poor Communication. Lack of Road Connectivity *et al*.

The wretchedness has robbed the aura of long icicles sighting around after a long spell of years. Years have gone down so swiftly but quality of life in Kashmir seems treading very slowly. It's pathetic and shameful as well. Even underdeveloped nations don't live like this. They too have some basic minimum standard of living.

Decade after decade, people have developed a sort of inertia to all these happenings in winter, one leading to other and so on. They are totally bereft of any institutionalized contingency plans to mitigate the effects of prolonged bad weather and instead their administration is only seen in *knee-jerk reaction* mode doing the proverbial *balancing act*. Meetings are convened to take *stock of situation*: 'stock position is satisfactory; some 40 odd machines for clearing snow are in waiting; so and so gas cylinders are in store; so much Kerosene oil is dumped, *blah blah*'.

However, in reality, nothing seems to have been in place. The high talk of cosmetic administrative reforms and so-called e-governance sounds as a big cruel joke for poor people of Kashmir, whom even the harsh winter leaves alone to suffer.

May be for outsiders winter in Kashmir means joy, nature's delight. For insiders, it means darkness. In every way.

18

DANCE ON ROADS

Your land. The realm of beauty and charm. I was rarely called for accomplishing the task assigned to me at this place. But to my utter surprise, nowadays I hardly get a breathing space here. Primarily, because of the people here and then those at the helm of affairs who have failed to ponder over the startling issue. At other places no sooner my stay prolongs, measures are rapidly taken to push me away. The casual attitude of people augmented with official apathy towards this nerve-racking matter scared me even. However, I was anxious to know the reason for this atypical scenario. And thus, I moved amidst the masses.

"You need not come for a second trial. Give us some *chai pani* and your license will be at your door step." I found one of the agents telling to his client who had failed to drive properly in the driving trial. This was the first shocker for me at the outset of my journey. Rather than honing his driving skills before getting license to drive, he was offered the license to kill.

"Make way. Keep away"! I saw some men in uniform shouting from their vehicle and whistling an incessant horn on the jam packed road. As a result of panic alarm, while trying to make way for their fast zooming vehicle, a car hit one pedestrian who was then rushed to the hospital. It was not the only security vehicle doing so. From every police and army vehicle to escorted civil officers' cars, public had to make way for them on congested roads. I was stunned to see that this behavior of security agencies and others only added to chaos and confusion, rendering roads more unsafe. At many of the places, I saw traffic managers making way for these 'special vehicles', and leaving rest of the public traffic in fuss. I thought to tell them that managing traffic is entirely different from managing law and order or appeasing those having power. It needs a distinctive outlook and expertise. Alas, I was not heard!

Saddened and incensed, I escaped to wider roads but all in vain. I was taken aback to see a speeding high-model bike with three school boys wearing no crash helmets. "It doesn't seem to be a place to perform aerobics on a bike, that too by the teens who are not entitled to drive", no sooner I muttered, I saw a pacing tinted glass luxury sedan driven by an adolescent overtaking another car hazardously. Thud. I heard a loud noise and reached the spot. The lavish vehicle had rammed over the divider and smashed into the car coming from opposite direction. "It is the neo-riche parents who are to be blamed", said an ambler on the spot, while I helplessly performed my job.

Frustrated, I decided to set out for outskirts and boarded a *Sumo*. Although the driver had a permit for to carry just seven passengers, he not only embarked ten people but even adjusted one on his seat. I was astonished to see that no one travelling in the *Sumo* objected to it. Anyhow, he left for his destination. From surpassing other vehicles perilously to crossing the speed limits on roads, the driver did not adhere to a single traffic rule. More or less, same scene was visible in other passenger-vehicles as well. The loaded tippers and load-carriers plying on the freeway didn't illustrate a different picture.

From open manholes to unaccomplished topping up, most of the roads over here were poor and had a shaky course. On scantily illuminated roads, I could hardly see warning/safety sign boards and proper colour demarcation. I saw the uncaring pedestrians, crossing roads negligently, untroubled about anything around!

All of a sudden, the *Sumo* was stopped by some traffic managers. "You are driving so recklessly and carrying lots of passengers. Come down and show me the papers", shouted one of the traffic personnel furiously. I felt glad for I thought the driver will be punished for his transgression. But I saw the fellow coming back cheerily, after he had some secret chat with the traffic managers. I was dumbfounded to see him driving as he was earlier.

Miraculously, I reached my goal. It was a beautiful health resort. I was happy to see people freaking out there. Later in the evening, it was raining heavily. The visibility was low. I was informed that two youngsters were on a car race and driving recklessly. As my task profile, I took away the soul of few of them. During the first five months of a year across the valley, I have already taken toll of 104 people in 717 road accidents. Yes, I did it. I had to. I am *Death*. And no holds barred, I am dancing on your roads. Without break off!

19

THE MYSTIFYING MUSE

Ghalib is easily and quickly reached. Why not! For he is among the very few who provide replies to many disquieting queries. His *Dewaan* (collection) usually lies around the corner. His *Dil Hi Tow Hai Nasang-o-Khisht (Its heart, not a small rock)* is my favorite. And if it is blended with Jagjit's dulcet voice, then there is no darling.

I wonder how Ghalib's *Muse* could fashion such a literary symphony so meticulously. It is not simply the toil of a thinking brain and a sensitive heart but also something divine that makes Ghalib really *Ghalib* (Overwhelming). That's why it's always bracing to recall—

Huvi Mudet Ki Ghalib Mar Gaya, Par Yaad Aata Hai,
It's been a while since Ghalib died but I still remember
Woh Her Ek Baat Par Kahna "Ki Yu Hota Tow Kya Hota"?

His love of argument, always saying: 'Fine, but if this had happened, then what"?

Almost all great poets and writers seem to possess an extra thing : godly aptitude. Almighty is generous towards them. They craft masterpieces and turn immortal. They become example for others. Of course, their *Muse* is extra-ordinarily fine and superior. John Keats writes about them—

> *Bards of Passion and of Mirth*
> *Ye have left your souls on earth!*
> *Have ye souls in heaven too,*
> *Double-lived in regions anew?*
> *Yes, and those of heaven commune*
> *With the spheres of sun and moon . . . .*
> *Thus ye live on high, and then*
> *On the earth ye live again;*
> *And the souls ye left behind you*
> *Teach us, here, the way to find you,*
> *Where your other souls are joying,*
> *Never slumbered, never cloying.*
> *Here, your earth-born souls still speak*
> *To mortals, of their little week;*
> *Of their sorrows and delights;*
> *Of their passions and their spites;*
> *Of their glory and their shame;*
> *What doth strengthen and what maim:-*
> *Thus ye teach us, every day,*
> *Wisdom, though fled far away.*

I don't know why but it seems I am frantically searching for my own *Muse*. I don't claim to be any

79

budding poet or a promising writer. How can I be!!
Being an ordinary student of Journalism, writing
is just a part of my profession. It is an obligatory
exercise. There is little scope for sounding creative.
What I write gives me just the feeling of being alive
to myself and to happenings around me, and nothing
else. It cannot qualify to be a part of active and pure
journalism. It's simply an adjunct of interpretation
and perspective, but forms the reactive and important
part of journalism, especially the contemporary
one. My humble opinions and impressions make
my columns. I'm not 'fortunate' enough to have
a Godfather to promote me by chiseling my raw
jottings. Neither do I've the 'privilege' of knowing
any Ghost Writer to write for me and add bylines to
my credit.

I confess there is no great writer within. My
language is not rich. It fills the columns as it comes
to me. I don't brag of any particular writing style.
Communication is the sole purpose, but not for every
reader. What I write may be lucid to a very few and
quite baffling for many. Nobody writes for everybody.
There is a segregated audience for different things in
each newspaper or for that matter any TV channel. I
never read Business or Sports Pages. It is not meant
for a finicky reader like me because it is not my cup
of tea. I occasionally go through Jug Suraya's *Jugular
Vein* or Shobha De's mumbo-jumbo. But I also know
that they won't stop writing simply because I am not
able to get them! They enjoy a huge class of admirers
and are established names in Indian literary circles.

And then, there is the all-pervasive question of
popularity. Some columnists write mainly for being

noticed and talked about. To write oddity and pour scorn on big names is their compulsive passion. For others, it's a mere compulsion to get a byline somehow. Yet, for a few others it is a calling by putting their viewpoint forward, least bothering about public prominence or recognition. They are unsung people; unknown to their own people. The selective readership of few people is gratifying for them as their writings are eventually sold to renewable garbage pickers. Mind it, the writers belonging to this category are not language masters or diction translators. They are not prize or award winners. Their *Muse* is their Conviction; their Belief that world will never go nuts altogether; Reason will never be dead; and catholicity of attitudes will never be bushed.

Without debate, in our times it's an unavoidable harsh reality that mediocrity attracts undeserved accolades and merit invites unwanted envy and cynicism. This is the rule of life. Success wins you true enemies and false friends. Rather it makes the distinction bare and clear. Your 'admirers' become your adversaries. Your 'friends' your critics. Your 'mentors' your competitors. Your 'teachers' your notorious rivals. Your 'dear ones' your dreaded ones. All discourage you to extreme. Doors of opportunity and expression are shut up on you. Leaving no stone unturned to show you down, they keep up their appearances. Their inflated egos and self-centeredness tries to hit upon your Achilles' heel. You become an eyesore, and a policy of exclusion is experimented upon you. What a pitiable joke! Failure gifts you sympathizers. Success takes all of them back. Perhaps this is what life is all about. No issues!

Coming back to the matter of *Muse*, I am at a wits end to learn, re-learn and de-learn many a truth or 'lesson'. I hear the frail voice of *Muse* emanating from somewhere. It tells me to stop treasuring anonymity, stop thinking about those who don't carry any weight.

My *Muse* also seems unhappy with me over being freezed in the troubled frame which is going just so and so. My *Muse* reprimands; it hauls over the coals—

The trouble is
You've kept yourself on too tight a rein,
Giving the most concrete of acts an abstract name.
Yes, I'm talking about the inner climax of your mind ~
The darkness, the occasional storms and hate
And wounding rains.
You think you can leave the nest
Without reason,
You think you know best?
Wouldn't you go
Wherever the wind takes you?
Of course, where ever you are,
Men will be persuading and estimating
They will be cynical.
But you could always pick a quarrel with the world,
Strike a combative posture without demur,
Treating serious matters with the frivolity they
deserve!
You could also confront the world
With a set of attitudes,

Keeping another set in reserve,
Thoroughly prepared in advance of course ~
Or you could be just brazenly precocious!
I tell you, if tired and spent, you may
Find succour in a sanctuary from clamour,
Where only the clocks tick and the dogs snore.
But even then, if people were to trouble you,
Come to me.
We'd take asylum in alien countries ~
Find imaginary homelands,
Look for desirable alternatives on prohibited trees!
But mind you, there would be raving storms,
And no place to rest,
And me craving to be a poet or a writer,
And you then, refusing to be so,
Would sing a swan-song for
Your songs were profaned.
But that would be only for a while.
And years, and years after years,
Gods would perhaps withdraw,
Or, betray their trust,
And maybe Time would offer no solace,
And then whether we cared or
Did not care
A Euripedes of a different race
Would sing of our serene despair.

20

CYCLE OF CRAVINGS

"This could not be the end of everything", he murmured while taking a deep sigh. With all despair and dismay on his face, he reclined back on his revolving chair. Restless and fearful, he was anxiously waiting for his senior assistant who was hastily called by his officers at the district headquarters. "Had I made a good deal with my life, apparently . . . ." he whispered. He recalled the day when he stepped into this profession in the capacity of the architect of nation. Yes, a teacher.

All his relatives and well-wishers had come to give blessings and good wishes to him when his name appeared in the selection list of teachers. His parents were full of pride for him. "Almighty has put a great responsibility on you, dispose off your duties accordingly", his humble father, a retired government servant, told him amidst the cheerful gathering at his home. "My son, I have amassed just one asset. It is a life of dignity and honor, and now you happen to be the custodian of my most precious belongings. Hold them close to your heart", he added.

Very soon, after his appointment as teacher, he was tied in a nuptial bond. Almighty graced him with three children. As time went by, his needs and desires saw a swell. He decided to construct a new house on the inherited piece of land. In the beginning when he started the work on his house, it was very difficult for him to make the both ends meet. However gradually, to the surprise of everyone, he did not only manage to construct a house, but he fixed every luxury to make the house look chic. He shifted to his palatial house and things started advancing at a fast pace. His children grew up and he made it a point to provide them all the comforts and conveniences. From paying hefty sum for coaching/tuition classes to buying latest gadgets of amusement for them, there was virtually no stop to endow the children with modern-day style of living.

In the meantime, he was promoted as a Head of one of the educational institutes. Naturally this marked a promotion of his life standard as well. Cars and bikes queued up in his compound. Garden lights and coloured iron-fences gave a classy makeover to ambience around him.

The time to surrender donation money for children's higher studies also passed off without hassles. The elder son obtained admission in a medical college outside the state. The only daughter took admission in a reputed private institute of management studies situated in a metropolitan. The youngest sibling was also enrolled for a professional course in one of the medical schools of South-Asian countries. He was successful in securing their careers with no trouble. Bucks had substituted the efforts efficiently.

One day the old father popped off. He was sad but not hurt. The drudgery of his material world saw his sane sentiments in shreds. His childhood memories had ditched him. He had no time for mourning. He was cleaved in worldly possessions. One desire mushroomed into various wishes. The cycle of cravings was expanding evermore. The comforts stockpiled. The opulence augmented. He was busy in planning and procuring more for his 'professional' progeny.

Time was flitting. Roses were quite rosy in his garden. Few years were left in his retirement but he was reluctant to retire. He wanted to play the splendid innings, slogging for affluence enormously. But the game was over beforehand. He had to leave the playing pitch, regrettably.

Without even knocking the door, his senior assistant barged in. Flashback fizzled. He was roughly rolled back in the present. The senior assistant uneasily told him, "Sir, a confidential letter for you". Like furling the pages of his bygone days, he hesitantly opened the letter just to read the subject as 'Suspension Order'. He was speechless.

In the evening, while watching the Urdu news channel, he was stunned to see a sting—news clipping showing a teacher heading an institute taking a 500 rupees bribe from the parent of a student. He couldn't believe his eyes. He buried his face in his hands.

21

DEPARTING WITH A MARK

He was watching a huge rush of people coming to their house. He spotted some people clearing the backyard of his house and few more persons helping them to burn firewood. He also noticed some of his relatives pitching the tent in their neighbor's lawn. Seeing all this, he quickly sneaked into his room and took some clean clothes from his messy cupboard. He wore them with enthusiasm as he felt that it was some occasion to celebrate. And while looking for her mother, he went into the gathering where he was surprised to see her lamenting. He put his hand over her face and asked naively, "Mom, why aren't you wearing new clothes? You see how many guests are visiting us".

The poor boy was too small to comprehend that it was the gathering over the demise of his father. The backyard was being cleared to perform his father's last rituals and tent was being pitched to accommodate the people for condolence. He greeted everyone who came in his way and guided the people to their respective places. Emotional outburst of the mourners was more for the innocence and gullibility of the small kid rather than for the deceased.

The family lived in an old dwelling. Dressed with raw mud, it had two rooms and some place for cooking. One really had to save one's head from whacking while entering the shabby rooms through fairly small doors. Light could hardly peep through the small openings in the rooms. The commodities in the cooking area were just hand-to-mouth.

"A nice soul has passed away, he had to struggle a lot. Fate has been so cruel to him", muttered one of the persons in the mourning assembly. He continued his talk, "His condition wasn't so earlier. Luck never favored him. He lost all his business assets, and then a young son . . . ."

"I don't think we have any right to comment on his fate and luck", interrupted one amongst the sitting crowd. Everyone around started to locate this defiant voice. It was an unfamiliar face. A frail old man with hump in his back, wearing silver beard, could hardly be noticed. "When he harboured no complaints against his fate and luck, who are we to do so?" the old man added. "I still remember the day he lost his elder son in an accident. I was looking for him. I heard his voice coming from behind the tree at a nearby place" the oldie narrated. He disclosed that as he went near the tree, he heard the deceased man saying, "Let all the adversities touch me. Let everything be taken away from me. You will still find me remembering You alone without doubting Your plan. I thank You for saving me from getting distracted from Your path by means of my children. I thank You for whatever You propose for me. You are the only Helper, the omnipresent and only omniscient".

Everyone in the gathering was listening to the old man very keenly. After a brief pause, he heaved a deep sigh and continued, "One day I found him very depressed. Those were the days when he had suffered a huge loss in his business. I extended my help but he denied, saying—"I am really worried as to why Almighty has given me only this much that I lost now?"

Before the old man could have thought anything else, he had added, "I wish that I had more riches, and whenever I would lose them, I would get an opportunity to thank Him".

The old man said that he was stunned on hearing this and thought to himself that these are the moments when Almighty Allah will be saying to His angels that this was *the reason* for making them prostrate before Adam (AS). With these words, the unfamiliar aged face left the tent.

Later, the little orphan kid wearing sparkling clothes was taken into the tent where people tried to convey him that his father was no more. "You see, your father has left this . . . ." Before someone could complete, the little boy replied confidently, "I know that my father is no more. You know just yesterday he was very jubilant. He was telling me that he was going to meet the One whom he loves the most".

The tiny boy had not suddenly turned precocious. He shared, "My father has advised me that neither for the fear of hell nor for the attainment of heaven, I should love Almighty because He is worth it and none besides Him can favor me. My death and life should be for Him".

The mourners were surprised since they could only see the old worn-out house as the indicator of the deceased's belongings and achievements, whilst his son was the genuine marker who knew that his father had departed with a different lesson.

22

THE SLEEPY KID

It's too early in the morning. Sun is still draped in floating clouds. Very few birds have begun chirping. Except a few stray dogs and a few persons lined up at baker's shop, the streets are deserted.

He is still in bed. In deep sleep. Enjoying the dreamscape of stories and characters he likes most. Frolicking in thoughts, unmindful of worldly worries, his eyes are weaving beautiful imaginings. A slight smile gets reflected from his innocent face, conveying he is relishing every second of his sweet sleep.

'Wake up, dear!' his mom cajoles him. The clock ticks gradually as he takes another turn, putting his back towards her. While as mom continues to caress him, he starts hiding his face with his pillow or pulling over his blanket to scroll under it sluggishly. He is not willing to leave his wonderful dreams unfinished. However, mom has no other choice but to wake him up against her own will. He tries hard to slip away from her arms, but she manages to lift him up. She hears the slow sound of words as he murmurs to himself, babbling different and funny dialects of his resentment. Mom just smiles and flatters his infantile ego.

Throwing all kinds of tantrums, he allows being taken to washroom for a face-wash. The moment the water drips down, he tries to escape and crouch again in the bed. The drama continues for some minutes. Eventually, he is fresh and takes few nips of milk, but with eyes half-shut, feigning he hasn't yet woken up completely. The drama continues. When the tantrums get too 'sleepy', the wet tissues and sipping straw help poor Mom to handle the master actor. Overall, the breakfast is messed and ultimately missed. A few scenes from *Doraemon* cartoon series stir him and Mom quickly starts putting on his school uniform while he is engrossed with his darling robo-cat. The clock is ticking faster. The whole home comes to a standstill. His dad settles his bag, granny prepares lunch-box, and grandpa combs his hair. So, the school bus is here! With his face pulled down, he sets off, waving his hand quite casually.

Every school-going morning is same. The little soul has no time to take delight in daily sunrise. Before the sun actually dawns, he is made to rise from his dreamy bed. He is made to behave mechanically, *ala* the animated robo-cat he likes to watch. And every Mom of such tormented kids has a same story to narrate.

Are all of us utterly helpless in re-christening the innocent infancy of our kids? As the childhood of our kids is getting packed down under the burden of so-called modern-day competition, its 'norms and demands', aren't the parents and teachers equally responsible for this unpardonable crime?

It's a pitiless affair. And, unscientific as well. In one of her articles titled '*The Early Bird Gets the Bad Grade*', Nancy Kalish, an internationally acclaimed journalist and author, observed—"For those still searching for a policy that might have a positive impact, here's an idea: stop focusing on testing and instead support changing the hours of the school day, starting it later for kids and ending it later for all children" *(The New York Times, 14 January—2008.)*

Similarly, Howard Taras, a professor of pediatrics at University of California-San Diego and who specializes in community pediatrics and school health, wrote in one of his research papers '*Poor Sleep, Poor Grades*'—"In a series of research articles, the relationship between children's performance in school and various health problems was examined. Of all the health problems investigated, poor sleep was among the most unexpected and definitive causes of poor academic achievement". Taras also writes that one of the reasons for this shortfall includes early school-start times.

Over here in Kashmir, the scenario is quite unusual. Without any proper research and findings, the government and other reputed private institutions claim to bring efficiency and competence through the mantra of 'morning timings' for the schools.

Astonishingly, the results cannot, at least, be craved for kindergarten where kids don't have to be pushed up for any academic battle. The innocent buds need time to bloom. They have to flower. We can't prod them to be gigantic trees. And that too, in a sleepy state!

But then, ironically, this is the way the general mind thinks about this issue. And the players involved are exploiting the same mindset.

23

PILLS THAT KILL

Half-heartedly, he was running after the people with his bank passbook. He actually wanted them to fill a withdrawal form for him. It was Saturday and bank was about to close. As such, no one had time to help him. However, seeing him worried, a young boy filled his withdrawal form.

"Please en-cash my form quickly. I have to pay for a diagnostic test tomorrow", he implored sadly to the banking associate.

Next day, he boarded the bus early in the morning to reach to the city centre in time. He had no other option but to repeat his CT scan from the imaging centre recommended by his doctor. With a big file of endless medical investigations, he visited his doctor. With all his curiosity and apprehension, he was looking at his doctor to hear some words of solace. While writing prescription after cursory look at the pile of reports, doctor said—"Here are some drugs, take them. Visit again after fifteen days". This was all he could listen from his doctor. Dejected, he left the chamber of doctor and bought the drugs. "Drugs for another fifteen days", was the only news he had for his inquisitive family members back home.

In spite of taking drugs religiously, the poor fellow could not find any improvement in his health status. And in fact, he gradually started remaining indoors as he was mostly keeping to his bed. It was also the spell when leaves on the trees were sapped and turning golden. No sooner the drugs prescribed by the doctor got consumed, more medicines were bought for him.

Now he couldn't really come out to work resulting in depletion of his savings. His miseries didn't stop here. In order to procure more drugs, he had to prematurely break his FD (fixed deposit) certificate that he had kept for his only daughter. It seemed that drugs are turning ineffective. His body showed puffiness in stage-wise and his colour turned pale with time. Outside, the trees could no longer bear the burden of writhing leaves. The gloom of the nights trounced over the extent of vividness of the days. The soothing morning breeze started turning into a fearful wind that ripped up whatever came its way.

The moment came when his family was left with nothing for procuring his medicines. The situation came to the brink of amassing money from the people in a local mosque during Friday congregations. Yet, something more was in store in the painful package of despondency for him. Two of his sons left their studies and geared up to be the bread-earners for their family. The daughter could not really spare any time from looking after her crippled father. His condition was worsening.

It was a nasty night for them. The puffiness had buried his eyes to the extent that he could not open them. He was losing his consciousness. All of a sudden, his daughter screamed. He had vomited blood. He was taken to nearby hospital. The preliminary measures proved ineffective in controlling his bleeding from mouth. He was referred to city hospital in the dawn. Lying down in ambulance, he felt he was heading aimlessly towards unknown and uncanny destination, leaving behind everything.

In the city hospital, he was rushed to emergency ward. After taking a comprehensive history and looking into the investigations he had done earlier, doctors were puzzled. They could not locate any condition that would lead to such an emergency. Anyhow, the attendants were told to arrange blood for the patient. Two of his sons hurried towards the blood bank to donate their blood. One of the senior doctors was consulted to start the treatment. While discussing the case with his juniors, he asked the attendants, "Can you show me the prescription and the medicines patient used to take?" The daughter passed on all to him, nervously. After a look, doctor took a long pause and said, "The manufacturing companies of these drugs are quite unknown and surprisingly these are not the actual medicines prescribed by the doctor. They have been replaced by some unfamiliar brand". Looking towards his junior doctors, he added desolately, "It is a spurious drug that has led to kidney failure in the patient complicated by a probable stomach ulcer that he was being treated for".

It was shock news. Everyone around was stunned. The deceit of some people had played with a precious life. His two sons came rushing with blood packs in their hands just to see their father motionless on the emergency trolley. Tablets of death had done the job.

24

MISFIT IN A MISSED WORLD

Blindly anonymous,
I couldn't find words
that could express me.
Downtown middle-class mentality,
nothing really remarkable
I have got!
The lines
that demand and
crave attention,
stagger to reason.
A dilemma
out of emotional miasma.
A sheer absurdity
spiced with
helplessness at the heart.
Frazzled and downcast,
I cease to ask for
some blonde hash,
some bogus antics.

*I refuse to buy
humiliation.
Anonymity became anonymous.*

Belonging to a middle class family, he had seen himself growing in an idiosyncratic downtown that had stoutly groomed many good characters as well as good customs. Inspired by them, he had imbibed certain resolute beliefs. His roots had existed as an interweaving factor to guide him in crucial decision-making in life. From opting for a career to choosing a spouse, he had grounded himself within those parameters.

He basked under criticism. 'Down-town middle class mentality': this was his impeachable brand quality. He would parade it proudly, and in return receive a verbal modicum of sarcastic approval.

Things were moving on nicely till increasingly awful congestion in downtown forced him to buy a small house in the so-called posh civil lines and settle there for good. A warm nestle of comfort was lost out. Initially, he did not stumble upon anything *'uncivilized'* about the new place. Rich people; palatial houses; brand cars; gaudy dresses; and of course, superficial smiles—it was an unknown world for him to get acquainted with.

The first nuisance dropped in. The next door landlady started to pop in often. The nagging woman was a leading gossiper who would spend hours with his better-half in the kitchen. Golden ornaments; lavish clothing; surplus money; social status—the vocabulary of kitchen was changing. 'Rebellion' was cooking up slowly. More precisely, it emanated as a *Kitchen Resistance*. The pushy wife became demanding and discontented. Making finicky comparisons was her habit now. This made him irritable and grumpy. He had never imagined that life will turn so glum and gloomy. A cheerless ambience had enshrouded him. The life beyond this life seemed to be a closed chapter as he found people around him rejoicing the rebellion against God. He was a misfit cruising in a missed world.

His means were adequate to lead a humble life; pompous lifestyle had no room there. Being a rank officer, he could have easily accumulated wealth through unscrupulous ways, but the conviction of his values always stopped him. His subordinates ridiculed him for being honest and termed his uprightness as 'Gullibility'. While he used to travel in public transport, they would come to office in private vehicles. Teasing him on petty matters or engaging him in trivialities, he was horrifically pressurized to adopt treachery and break his integrity. Corruption was so overruling and superseding that it took his mental toll to resist it. He experienced uncertainty as the conflict between what he believed in and what he saw in reality around, gave rise to a kind of a moral dilemma. He was between the devil and the deep sea. However, he knew that when values conflict, choices are to be made and thus, his strong will overpowered. This, notwithstanding the fact, that he was frequently transferred from one place to another, at times dumped in *Official Cells*.

Even the social circles were torturous and tormenting for him. He proved to be an odd one out. He failed to live up fallaciously. It was an ordeal to exchange and maintain social connections which had turned into simple 'liabilities'. He could not manage to spend extravagantly on various social occasions. Most of his relatives would look down upon him as a broke on the breadline. Nonetheless, he journeyed on.

Religion for him was not a ritual to celebrate. He wasn't a staunch believer but he won't exhibit his genuine fanaticism for public consumption. He meant *Faith*. Unflinching one. That's why he would vocally nullify anything reeled off without meaning or mere hypocrisy packed off in the name of religion. Gimmickry with humbug and empty religious rhetoric was unacceptable to him.

Nobody was happy with him. He would complain about a shopkeeper indulging in black marketing. He would argue with the bus driver for violating road rules and playing with the safety of passengers. He would object to 'unique' approach of youngsters towards their life. He would openly demur about the leaders failing in their task. He would protest against the crooked politicians who dupe naïve people. He would oppose anything that was morally and principally incorrect. People had named him unsolicited *'confrontationist'*: a crabby fellow spoiling for a fight!

He would also question the insensitivity on the part of his society, which was getting deep and serious. He was disturbed by the 'moral panics' of the society whose value-system was getting fragile and feeble to stand any moral weight. He was labeled as 'maverick' whenever he spoke his heart out. His thinking was blatantly scoffed at and it never surprised him. There was nothing tangible he could do to stop all this since there was a rising glorification and recognition of all this in the society. Values had taken a backseat and it was a state of complete collapse.

He retired as an ordinary official. No awards were conferred on him for his honest contribution. He had no *high contacts* to market his competence. A scarce pack of pension was the entire he got for slogging prime years of his life in upholding things which made him anonymous. But he carried no regrets. About anything.

25

CRUCIAL YEAR!

There were seven million wonders of the world in the eyes of this child. He was born into this world as a new thought of God, an ever fresh and radiant possibility. The only son of his parents.

His mother meticulously packed his lunch, water bottle and some spare clothes. *Honk! Honk!* No sooner he heard the horn, he holed up himself behind his grandma. He was unwilling to leave the warmth of her lap. However, he had no other choice but to board the crèche van with other toddlers.

Standing feeble on the back seat of the van, he innocently watched the agile humankind around him. He was unable to comprehend the purpose of his arrival in the world of light. Rather, he pined for the darkness of womb, where he rejoiced his nine long months stay.

Now, he would often hear his father saying to his mother—"This is the crucial year for preparing our son to face the interview for securing kindergarten admission in any of the leading schools." The little soul was wandering whether he shall start by uttering *Baba* or shall he mumble *Baa Baa black sheep* . . . the rhyme he learned in crèche.

He was in his formative age—the time to be molded softly. He was mulling over the dilemma of either learning the moral lessons of life from his grandparents in his mother-tongue or struggle mugging up *ABC* and *123* in order to conquer the 'competition' he was saddled with from day one. Of course, it was the time for him to learn the diverse aspects of life and get his personality shaped. However, most of the efforts of his parents were aimed at preparing him for the mad race. Perhaps, overbearing but concerned parents knew the wicked reality of the world waiting him outside—the one that thrived on worst kind of manipulation, treachery and fraud, and where high merit was vital to remain in race if one does not possess skill or knack of monkey business. The outer world was really brutal and bad.

So, he was fashioned into a 'proficient competitor' with doses of stress and strain layered over him. In this pursuit, his guardians somehow forgot to pass on to him the true beauty of life and the actual demeanor of his being. While worrying about what he will become tomorrow, they forgot that he is someone today. The tenderness of his soul was overlooked.

Three years later, his parents were delighted to see his name in the selection list of children admitted to the reputed school they had dreamt of. His parents were contended that their son will now get the best possible education to make a bright career. "My dear son, I am proud of you, put all your efforts to be topper in your every class; after all, these few years are crucial for you", his father told him gladly.

Crucial years gradually approached. He proved to be a submissive son, worked hard as it was ordained and never let his parents down. In the process of 'burning the midnight oil', his kiddish pranks and penchant also got seared. The child in him was lost. His childhood turned lifeless. Although he loved playing cricket, he couldn't play the game a great deal. He liked watching animated movies endlessly, but he was softly stopped for squandering his precious time. He was fond of reading comics and fairy tales, but he was gently made to give it up. The *do's and don'ts* were his companions. He was told that his eighth class exams were significant for him and he need to spend most of his time in studying.

After lot of studious work, he came up to the expectations of his parents and stood among the toppers of the Middle School Board Examination. This certainly raised the expectations of his parents. They aspired to see him in the top rank of class 10th exam results as well. From best tutors available in the city to best possible books, his parents provided him all the essential facilities. And all along he was often reminded that he had a crucial time ahead.

Devoting most of his time to studies, he would even prefer not to attend the marriage ceremonies of his relatives. Even if he would go, he was usually brought back after few hours and disallowed to stay overnight at any place. There was a strange and unseen pressure mounting on him. He was unable to express the uncanny unease that was slowly but surely depressing him. Yet, he concentrated on his studies and appeared in class 10th exam.

In the family and friend circle, he was considered as the most hard working, exceptionally intelligent and genuinely decent boy who breathed in his world of books. Pointing him as a role-model, lot of his relatives desired their children to be like him, seldom knowing that he was fashioned only to be the 'victorious entrant' into the stunning cutthroat world, oblivious of the basic veracity of his survival.

The 10th class results were declared. He had secured more than ninety percent marks, but had lagged behind the three toppers with just a margin of few marks. The congratulations poured in from all relatives and acquaintances. However, the mood in the family was damp. His parents were not happy. "It is a downslide. You were the first position holder all through your school; your brilliant performance so far has petered out. Anyway, the coming two years are now most crucial for your career. Start preparing to prove your mettle," said the disappointed father.

Some months passed. His parents had unwittingly left coercing him for his extensive studies. As usual, he used to remain indoors and study in his room. One evening, when he was having his dinner with the family, his father casually inquired about his studies—private tuitions, school classes, books, computer *et al*. He gave a brief reply to everything and went to sleep.

Next morning, it took him unusually much time to come down for the breakfast. His mother went to see him, only to find him literally lifeless in his tidy room.

The crucial year had finally come, and taken him far away. Forever. The little teen didn't grow up freely to be a caring friend of his Mom and Dad. He left eternally, making them painfully understand what life is all about while they had vainly tried to tutor him all about life.

26

Inspired to Izhar

"She is my cousin, take care of her", he said while introducing me to one of the faculty members of the varsity department where I had secured admission. It was not for the first time that he turned out to be a true help for me by seeing me at the place where I am today. He had been a source of encouragement and facilitation since the times when I used to post my hand-written manuscripts to *Daily Greater Kashmir,* of which he was a founder member. In fact, it was he who after having his Masters in Mass Communication & Journalism gave me an idea about this stream of study. He was the only one in our family to have pursued this subject.

Not just me, he was a source of inspiration for many other students and budding journalists who wanted to excel in the field of media. He inspired many of us to *Izhar*—to express ourselves for the greater good, to articulate with scrupulous impartiality, to be the communicators of reality.

I remember it was my first profile-writing assignment as a student and I was confused whom to contact and interview. I was reluctant in meeting anyone I didn't know. I called him up and he solved my problem. I succeeded in reporting my first profile. It was carried by the Lab journal of my department under the headline—*'Out of chaos, a dancing star: Izhar Wani'*.

One gloomy morning, some unknown sadness gripped me. I somehow started for the University when one of my relatives rang me up and said, "Do you know, Izhar has to undergo a surgery for treatment of a critical disease?" I had nothing to respond, nothing to express. Over some period, I lost track of Izhar and in the process, sorrowfully, lost him forever. It immensely hurts to recall that I could not be in constant touch with him. An occasional phone call or short message to enquire about his health was the only connect. In last text, he wrote: 'Keep praying for me'. He, for sure, knew that this was the only thing I was doing for him, from a distance away.

When Izhar was shifted to Sheri-Kashmir Institute of Medical Sciences (SKIMS) in a serious condition, I mustered courage to see him, finally. A frail body was struggling with grace. He opened his eyes for a fraction of second and did not say anything. He left many things unsaid. And he also left many things unheard. But with that agile glimpse, he subtly made his *Izhar*. He was conveying his worry about the apple of his eyes, his two wonderful daughters. He was relating to his brave parents whom he loved so much. And he was thinking about his better-half, whom he never wanted to be alone in the midst of a colossal tragedy.

I left the hospital with all obscurity, till I came to know that he had now nothing more to *Izhar*. I had hardly imagined that Izhar will prove to be a real dancing star, one day. The one that flickers even amidst the fatal chaos. The one that had the capacity to twinkle beyond the being.

Proving to be a courageous participant in the great play of life, Izhar was not just a simple passer-by. His quality work and good deeds cried for him. I remember when I profiled him, he said: "If you are going to be a tough and honest reporter and a good person, you have to be prepared to pay the price and not necessarily to expect a reward. You do the job for its own sake, because it is right thing to do. Ultimately, that protects you".

Of course, he protected himself. He was excellently able to protect *Izhar*. As a result, his integrity and credibility also got protected.

However, we the mortals could not protect him from the clutches of Death. We have lost a great friend, a great journalist.

His demise has brought home a harsh lesson about not staying in touch with our near and dear ones, for we never know that the moment we are with them may turn out to be the last moment. We need to be with them before we lose them. Forever.

Today, I am again profiling him. But this time he is not around to give me inputs. Even the phone connect is gone. This can't be his obituary. It sounds painful.

Pray we protect and preserve the values he stood for, all along. That can be the best tribute in his everlasting memory.

27

ROOTS NEVER DESERT

I have only one friend in south India. She's a Software Engineer. Being talented and creative, she has a penchant for poetry and even writes good poems. Some months back, she gifted some of her poetic pieces to me. I liked them awfully and treat them as her keepsake. Her nascent experiences and promising emotions expressed in a plain style impressed me a lot. Some of her poems are cathartic. One of them is about her stay in a college hostel situated very far away from her home. Inspired by a famous poem of English literature, the poem titled *Those Promises Made* is a touching bit that made many of hostlers' in her college to make huge pin-ups of it and hang it on their hostel room walls—

The wind playing with
my unbraided hair.
I reflect on the day
I left my home

for wisdom so small.
Tracing untrodden ways
on my own, Nothing to guide me
but my father's say.
Like little Red Riding Hood
through the jungle.
Lots of jackals,
lots of hunters on my way.
Endure all this
I say to myself.
For I have promises to keep.
As I was leaving my doorstep,
Mother says 'Baby,
take care of yourself'.
Dad with a stern look
Says 'it's time to say goodbye'!
Hiding behind his stern looks,
He must have dropped a tear
and said, 'My little princess
will come back a grown girl'.
But for this and nothing
more I have promises to keep.
For nothing but the confidence
invested in me.
Armed with this and
a goal to reach.
I gather memories as
they are shed.
Like autumn leaves
on a windy day.
And I sit to work.
As I have promises to keep . . . .

(Mariam Tareen)

113

How queer is it indeed to leave your home for a goal that seems quite small in value than the love you enjoy at home! Nonetheless, we leave and leave with a difference. Nostalgia and melancholy accompanies us. Roads seem unfamiliar and untried. Faces obscure and strange. Tasks challenging and taxing. Amidst all this mushy sense, we are reminded of things sacred and trusty. Something rejuvenates our mood and morale. Those words that ring. Precepts that inspire. Feelings that heal. Trust that supports. Evermore. Always.

The 'Little Princess' who lives like Alice in wonderland, unmindful of her age and era, suddenly feels grown up and serious. The frivolities of childhood look silly. Troubling Mom and Dad becomes sore. Playing pranks with brothers appears odd. Out of the blue, she realizes that she's a changed person. Little success and small ambitions rob her of all fund. She now behaves and bothers.

'We know you'll do it'—her dear and near ones boost up her spirit. Artless Mom says all in silence. Her teary eyes bid adieu in simmering sobs and prayers. From bags to baggage, she meticulously arranges everything. The amulets she brings secure her baby. Dates and sugar balls from various shrines safeguard her against bad health. Mom feels satiated about this 'precautionary' homework. Her baby is leaving the nest and is on the wings.

Dad offers ideas and instructions. He recites Holy Scriptures for her safety and honour. The little babe he overprotected and over cared enormously was moving out alone for the first time. He permitted though half-heartedly. He never wanted her to go so far. Never. But the trust and hope he had invested in her over a long period of her upbringing, made him feel at ease. He knew she'll come back with dignified distinction. A man of high ideals and principles, his daughter wasn't a patch to him. She couldn't be what he actually wanted her to be in life. And she held this regret for all time. She recalls *Marvi*, a serial telecast from Pakistan Television (PTV) many years back. A simple girl from arid village, *Marvi*, leaves for metropolitan city for higher studies. The first letter she receives from her father opens with the touching words—"Dear, what kind of father I am? I have let you go in the ocean of crowd! But I am sure you'll find your shore and save yourself for no one but me". The 'little princess' also hears her father saying so tacitly.

The portraits of departed grandparents in her room relate to her every day. Their tender love had spoiled her. Grandpa was happy with her as usual. He was always proud of her. Grandma was her foster mother. From packing lunch for her school to collecting her result cards, she was available for everything. The charming shades of joint family and its loveable shield had instilled the little babe's world. If only the pictures on the walls of her snug room could breathe and decode her communication!

Seasons have changed. Alice is no more Alice. The birdie is no more birding. Wonderlands are preposterous. Nests are uncanny. Emotions coloured her. Maturity has prepared her. The whiff of warmth around her made her. But the voyage to world outside is enigmatic. Those pledges; those vows. A few with herself, many a lot with others. All remind her of something worth remembrance. Her people. Their plight. Gore. Mayhem. Bleeding hearts. Bruised psyches'. The unending tale . . .

What's to be left behind? Reminiscences? Recollections? Joy? Pain? Everything? Exactly what? . . . . The roots pull her. Someone perhaps calls out there. It's a feeble voice from somewhere. It emanates from faintly treasured thoughts and vaguely cherished ideals. Who's out there? She shrieks as the time flings her into new realm.

Is it far to go? A step no further. It is hard to go? Ask the melting snow. The Eddying feather. What can I take there? Not a hank, not a hair. What shall I leave behind? Ask the hastening wind. The fainting star. Shall I be gone long? For ever and a day. To whom there belong? Ask the stone to say. Ask my song . . .

Cecil Day-Lewis

Mom holds her and caresses. Dad stands behind and supports. The 'Little Princess' sheds her all but those promises . . . She'll come back a grown girl. Hopefully!

28

LIFE'S JOURNEY

Working hard for many years altogether, he had dogged tirelessly to see his dreams come true. He had put all his efforts to come out as a successful candidate in the interview he had appeared in. He availed all his sources and quarters to figure in the selection list. He utilized his complete resolve to be through.

"I knew I'll get the appointment letter and visa. After all I had struggled passionately to achieve this goal", he yelled with delight, while reading out the selection letter. It was only after a series of exams and health checks, he got qualified for the job abroad. He shared the news with his parents and friends. He had to reach embassy within two days to submit his passport. As the airfare was too expensive for him, he decided to drive his father's car to Delhi accompanied by his friend. Though his parents were reluctant in letting him do so, he somehow convinced them, and started his journey one fine morning.

That day he woke up early. After having his bath and breakfast, he assured his mother that he can drive well, and so she should not worry. He left his home while his mother watched him till his car was out of her sight. In the city outskirts, he asked for a brief safety inspection of his car.

"This is the famous green channel posed between firm tall poplar trees", said his friend, soon after they crossed *Sangam* bridge. Everything appeared green and soothing to him. Apparently, he was at peace, quiet and calm. But somewhere down his heart, he was longing for some unknown serenity. He was a bit anxious.

While fuelling up his car at a filling station, a disabled person on wheel chair appeared in front of his window. He was selling colourful dusting cloth. In spite of having one in his car, he bought the dusting cloth, choosing the brightest coloured in the lot. "You didn't need it, you should have simply refused", said his friend to him. "He was disabled, yet he was not begging. I just tried to boost his morale", he replied moodily.

They had to wait for few minutes before they entered *Banihal* tunnel. No sooner they entered in, an absolute darkness stemmed. The shadowy passage reminded him of his gloomy days before receiving the appointment letter. He put on the headlights of his car for an appropriate view, and hastily asked his friend, "Did you perceive the out-and-out darkness when we entered the tunnel? My life was similarly so two days ago". The jolly good friend just nodded.

Travelling down the nippy low-lying clouds and picturesque meadows, he seemed contended. He was thinking of a future where he can now settle down nicely and get a bride of his liking. While steering gradually through scenic lush green valleys, he planned of providing best moral ethics and education to his children. Reaching to the crisscrossed peaked highway, he also thought of taking proper care of his parents in their old age.

The ambiance appeared all in his favour. But again, deep inside, he sensed some flatness. Anyhow he continued with his journey. Moving fast through the smoggy and crammed access roads during night, he somehow managed to reach the embassy next day morning.

Fatigued and sleepy, he survived the deadline and got his visa and work permit. His friend bid him smiling adieu as he boarded his flight to continue his voyage. Flying high in the skies, he dreamt of living a sky-scraping life. There were so many dreams travelling alongwith him.

He joined his workplace and as usual carved a niche for himself through his competence. His employers were all praise for him. The dedication towards his profession made him to advance and excel, and he was promoted to next position only after one year.

Back home, his parents started looking for an appropriate match for their son. They chose a bride for him. He came back after two years. His parents were delighted to see their son as a prosperous and complete person. He solemnized the marriage with the girl of their choice in a simple way. He performed *Nikkah* in a local mosque and took the bride to his home.

Embarking upon newly married life, he was trying to develop a loving relation with his wife, and gradually both of them began to love each other very much. Before coming back home, he had applied for the family visa for his wife.

One morning, just a few days after his marriage, he got up quite early and went to his parent's room. "What are you doing here?" inquired his mother in panic. "I do have everything. I achieved whatever I aspired of. I thank you for everything. But Mom, something is missing somewhere", he uttered despondently, with a strange worry on his face. "I think you are missing your workplace. Don't worry, try to complete all the documentation formalities soon. But for today, you need to remember that we have been invited over lunch by your in-laws" said his mother, brushing off his unexplained anxiety with a caring smile.

All was set. He along with his wife and parents started preparing for the invitation. He was visiting his in-laws for the first time. His wife was glad. All her relatives were eagerly waiting to see him.

Setting out, all of them boarded the car he drew. After only few minutes, he stopped the car on a roadside and chokingly cried out, "I am not feeling comfortable. I am feeling acute pain within . . . ." and collapsed down instantly.

The shocked father drove him directly to the nearby hospital. After a brief examination the doctors diagnosed him "Brought Dead".

The young groom stumbled on what he was mysteriously missing all through: The angel of death that hovers over all of us but a very few sense him.

CONTRADICTION

29

DILEMMA DISTRESSING

The night was cold. He wasn't feeling well. Inspite of the shivering cold, he woke up in the morning to offer prayers in the nearby Shiv temple. Dawn wore a gloomy look. The ambience seemed atrocious. He could see nothing but thick smog that irritated his eyes. It was unusual; he had not heard *Adhan* from the mosque situated on way to Shiv temple. As a mark of reverence and veneration, he used to bow his head the moment he passed by the mosque. This he had been doing since years.

However, this was an atypical dawn. As he was nearing the mosque, he witnessed few people talking loudly on the roadside. He wore his glasses with his frail hands just to see a plain ground with a tin board painted "DDA Property" at the site of mosque. He was shocked and equally confused, and with a sense of profound grief he hugged the *Muezzin* of the mosque, his old pal, and whispered—"This is not fair, it should not have happened in the country of Gandhi and Azad. I feel sorry". The aged *Muezzin* replied poignantly—"Without letting us know anything about it, these DDA (Delhi Development Authority) people have grounded this mosque and took the debris away during night hours".

That bleak morning, Ram Lal did not go for worship to Shiv Temple. He couldn't move beyond the rubble. He stayed back with the people at the demolished mosque and networked to gather more people from his community to show solidarity with the enraged group. Gradually, the crowd began swelling and people from various parts of Delhi assembled near the site of demolished mosque. However, the scene did not turn ugly as it was not something that could have incited inter-community tension. People demonstrated matchless communal harmony and unanimously voiced their disapproval over the DDA action.

Ram Lal alongwith a few members of the mosque committee went to DDA office. He was disgusted and furious. A weird kind of mood weighed him. On entering the office of the concerned officer, Ram Lal folded his hands and started humbly—"Sir, I am witness to Indian independence and partition as well. At the time of partition, I persuaded and held back many of my Muslim friends from migration. It was simply by giving them assurance about their safety and religious freedom . . . ." He was brashly interrupted by the officer—"The religious structure was built illegally on DDA land and was demolished after a committee approved it". Ram Lal retorted back—"I am a freedom fighter, and we have given tremendous sacrifices to build this nation, the one that is presently meshed up in scams and scandals. Corruption and dishonesty has eroded the sanctity of this country. Can we afford more tensions at this juncture? You should have exhibited some sense of sensitivity over this issue". "But we had court orders to do so", answered the officer. "Look my dear, you could have issued notice of demolition to the mosque committee before actually knocking down the mosque", Ram Lal said to the officer and added—"I have been seeing this mosque standing there since many years, and as far as I know, the religion of Islam does not allow any mosque to be built on encroached or illegally occupied land; not even a single brick that has been acquired illegally can be used in its wall". The officer was unmoved, turning a deaf ear to all his words, and in fact sneered at Ram Lal consistently as he was speaking.

Disappointed and disillusioned, Ram Lal put his head down in dismay and left the office. He reached home with unease surrounding him glaringly. He lied down on his bed, lost in strange thoughts. "Baba, you had nothing since morning, have a cup of tea", said his daughter. Before he could hold the cup, a loud thud rocketed outside. A clatter of something like a blast scared them. It was a tear gas shell fired on the protesters who were protesting the demolition of mosque. "People haven't yet forgotten some historical blunders. And this country is breeding more hatred and hostility. Radical mind-set is getting strong. How unfortunate", Ram Lal said, while peeing through the windowpane, to his daughter.

Next day morning, Ram Lal couldn't wake up early. There was no *Adhan*. The whole locality was sunk in silence. Glancing through the morning newspaper, he read out the front-page news that reported, "Mosque demolition causes protests, jams: Jangpura, near Nizamuddin in southeast Delhi, virtually turned into a mini-battlefield on Wednesday with riot police lobbing teargas shells and wielding lathis to disperse a large number of people protesting against the demolition of a mosque . . . ." (*Daily Times of India, 13*th *Jan—2011)*.

"Unwarranted, uncalled for", Ram Lal murmured while scanning the rest of the newspaper. He preferred to stay back at home, and have a time off for nothing.

A few days later on one morning, Ram Lal's daughter came running and jubilantly said to him—"Mosque will be rebuilt! Baba, see the newspaper". With a bit of agility and astonish, he read the headline, "Faced with protests, CM pledges to rebuild mosque". The newspaper had reported that "Chief Minister blamed the DDA for acting in an unfair way by demolishing the mosque without letting the Delhi Wakf Board present its case before the court. CM had also sent a note to the Prime Minister apprising him about the situation" (*Daily Times of India, 15*th *Jan—2011.)*.

Ram Lal wasn't amused. Dropping the newspaper, he snickered and muttered, "This can happen only in India . . . . *Mera Bharat Mahan*!

30

'. . . . FOR THE SAKE OF YOUR RAMZAAN'

Sudden smash to smithereens. The sound was shattering. Everyone around stood horror-struck. It was breaking of a big windowpane. The glistening pieces of glass were splintered on the floor. It appeared like a real time trailer from a movie.

No sooner I tried to gather myself in one of the famed readymade garment outlets, few furious youth barged in. They instantly started abusing the administrators of the store. Caring a damn about the presence of scores of children and females around, the enraged youth used foul language and brutally banged the sales personnel of the store.

The ambiance turned chaotic as well as astounding. An abrupt panic gripped everyone. In trepidation, the people snuggled up their children in the interiors of the store to save them from stampede. Instantly, the salespersons of the store removed their Identity cards and holed up themselves in various washrooms in order to save themselves from getting thrashed up gratuitously. Briskly, the shutters of exit and entry points of the store came down fast. All the customers got stuck inside.

"Get that person, where is he . . . ." I heard one agitated youth shouting. He was frantically looking for one of the male staff members posted at the exit gate of the store who had allegedly frisked the handbag of a certain female customer "in a bad way". In a jiffy, I saw people rushing towards one egress to escape from the maddening scene. But, someone from outside dashed to stairs the pigeonhole wooden cabinet used for keeping the belongings of customers prior to their entering the store. The same knocked over the scared customers, injuring a few of them. And deafeningly, the stuff in the cabinet speckled the whole floor.

Seeing this, some people started running away in panic, whilst some rushed towards the spot to gather their belongings for which they had got a valid plastic token. Surprisingly, a few customers started picking up others' bags dotted on the floor. As situation was getting worse, I sheltered myself behind one concrete wall. I anxiously watched people moving from one place to another, ransacking everything that came their way.

"Tear the price tag and wear this full sleeve on your T-shirt", I heard someone saying on the other side of wall where I was hiding. I atrociously peeped through a small opening in the wall and saw some people ripping the tags of garments kept in display and wearing them over their clothes. Taking advantage of the situation, I even caught sight of some females walking off with clothes sling in the hangers and burying them under their veil (*Burka*).

"Leave me! I am innocent, I have done nothing, I don't have knowledge of anything; I was sitting in the office, I swear by your *Ramzaan* (Islamic month of fasting); please don't thrash me for the sake of your *Ramzaan*", I heard someone pleading desperately in a non-Kashmiri accent. I tried to come to the end of the wall. I noticed few youth dragging one non-Kashmiri person who happened to be the Manager of the store. Fright and sense of vulnerability was visible in his eyes. His store was plundered. Violently. He was looking defenseless, alone and scared, and that too in the holy month of *Ramzaan* amidst 'Muslims'. More so, when he was not proved guilty! Without ravaging his store, the matter could have been sought in a peaceful manner, I thought to myself.

Meanwhile, I spotted some people hastening towards the exit gate that had gone open. Without any delay, I too sneaked out from the store. I was taken aback to see some police personnel alongwith a police officer, watching the whole pandemonium as mute spectators. Hurrying towards the main road, I also saw one person holding a brand new cloth in his hand and saying proudly to his friend, "You see this piece, it was priced for rupees 775. In this pell-mell, I replaced its price tag and managed to buy it for just rupees 195".

The store was burgled. I heard people making stories outside the store. Some were labeling it as a "Planned rampage" by hired hooligans and others were taking sadistic pleasure out of the whole ruckus.

Back home, I was thinking about hundreds of Kashmiris' who earn their livelihood outside, in canvas laden bamboo stalls on the beaches of Goa to big showrooms on the landscape of Hampi. What if, God forbid, similar situation evolves for them?! What is it they will plead their life over? And will anybody listen to them?

I had no simple answers.

31

INADVERTENTLY, WE CONVEY!

Neither nice words nor long speeches depict the actual within any individual. Behind the charade of verbosity and fluency, we easily impress others and satisfy our inflated egos. That's why verbal communication is a great art, brimmed with all the nuances of world mastery. However, non-verbal communication or what is known as kinesics includes no art but is a spontaneous and uncensored exposition of our behaviour. This non-verbal behaviour always communicates. We convey inadvertently. At times, it proves to be a dead giveaway. So, there is always a "non-verbal leakage" from each one of us through our non-verbal communication, revealing what we really are.

Few months back, I had a chance to attend the book release function organized by some custodians of 'dying' art and culture. The chief guest, a leading light of society, had a terrible "non-verbal leakage". It was damn hot that day, and unluckily in the midst of philosophical deliberations, there was an abrupt power cut, bringing all the ceiling-fans at the venue to a grinding halt. Everybody present was perspiring including the honorable chief guest. Waiting for nothing, he quickly removed the attached book jacket (paper cover) of the copy of the released hard-bound book which was gifted to him. He folded the book jacket and fanned it out for agitating the air to cool himself. Whether the star turn of the function did it deliberately or not, but the non-verbal communication from him smacked of plain intellectual snobbery.

The book authored after deep and extensive study by a learned scholar, deserved reverence and accolades. But, unfortunately, it seems that those who speak loud don't perhaps know that small actions speak louder than big words. There is no labouring required to crack on for hours about religion, reform, and intellectual awakening. But there is certainly the need for strenuous efforts where an individual can prove the veracity of his words through his deeds.

It is not being sarky about the intellectual stalwarts of this piece of bruised land, who after being witness to a gory mayhem, have come out of hibernation to jangle on the clichéd art and culture of the walking wounded who buried thousands of precious human brains under the soil of oblivion. In fact, the walking wounded of our land owe a deep 'gratitude' to such coterie of great *Avtaars* for their courtesy to dabble in hyperbole and have a whole of a time here.

Recently, while wading through the pages of one newly launched magazine 'The Kashmir Impact', a long poem in its literary dispatch column was a perfect musing. Titled as *'Long Live Intellectuals'*, it was a critical verse of ponderings. Addressing the same *Avtaars,* the poet writes—

Selling your intellect cheap to the State,
You deserve to be remembered with Hate
If you don't have the nerve to stand and speak, For
justice and truth
Break your Pen, burn your Book, it is real Justice to
you as a sloth.

(Mushtaq Sikander)

Back to my observation which has a possibility of being dismissed as beside the point, the fact remains that it is through insignificant matters that most of us show what we are made of. We demean ourselves so poorly. 'Intellectuals' are no exception. As said by Arthur Schopenhauer, "Individuals best show their character in trifles, in trivia where they are not on their guard. It is in the simplest habits that we often see the boundless egotism which pays no regard to the feelings of others and denies nothing to itself".

32

REAL CONSERVATIONISTS!

Come winter and it is examination fever gripping the students all over. Dull looks, long-drawn faces, unkempt hair/beard and absolutely no *make-up* are the salient characteristics of students these days. Well, going a step ahead, some of them remain absolute *WOB's (with-out-bath)* for days together. Of course, it goes to show their concern for building a bright future and a better tomorrow. Nothing wrong there. In fact, in the process they also save their Dad's bucks by adhering to *WOB* norm by consuming no soap and no shampoo. They, at the same time, conserve a small amount of petrol utilized in their bikes/cars for roaming all through the academic year. They even conserve mobile and internet bills for their parents, to some extent.

So, it's just another moving example of conservation of 'resources'. You have conservation of wildlife; conservation of forests; conservation of Dal-Lake; conservation of water; conservation of power; conservation of fuel and what not. Please add conservation (hoarding) of onions, potatoes and tomatoes also.

Just the other day, one of my friends was explaining to me the nuances of difference between reservation and conservation. "Simple!", she said, "reservation is a political slogan meant for vote-catching and conservation is a slogan—official, public or individual—meant for ballyhoo and some aggrandizement even though denied vociferously."

What an 'eco-friendly' and 'environ-aware' theory she had put before me, even as I was thinking about those fly-by-night activities and promises of their Yo-Yo sponsors who have *naturopathy, homeo and herbal* methods to tackle every problem. Well, looks like our politico-bureaucratic recipe:

Winter—it's so cold here.

No problem! Move to Jammu.

Electricity is erratic.

No problem! Don't use geysers and heat blowers, look at the bulb and that should be enough to warm you up.

But see the dilapidated roads.

No problem! Why should you move in cold? Move to warm areas or remain confined until weather is okay.

O! this public transport, can't you improve it?

No problem! Winter vacations and *Durbar-Move* will lighten their load and there will be no overload.

But that garbage is piling up.

No issues! It won't stink during winters.

And those street dogs?

Ridiculous, you seem ignorant of animal rights.

Then what about human rights?

What the hell! Can't you do anything yourself. After all, we (in government) also have a *Family-Life*.

Says a bureaucratic oldie—"You see these people here have these nagging habit of asking for this and that all the time. Just allow us to have a gala time until April and then, no problem, we will try to set things right."

So then, conservation of *guts and vocal chords* is the name of the game until the *Durbar* is back. Lick it or lump it, but that's it.

Coming back to exams, our students even though they become *puritanical* conservationists during exam time, are not able to show good results (majority of them). Why? Simple theory! You see they work hard throughout the year in the name of *Masti* and wiping out their *Hasti* from Polo View to Palladium. Being virtually on cloud nine, they spend their time mostly in *Sapnoo Ki Basti* (Dreamland). How come can they remember so many things—there's so much to assimilate from Friends to Facebook. And why not? Even my kindergarten son sings '*Kuin Ki Her Ek Friend Zaroori Hota Hai'*. Their *Hard Disks* always brimming. Complete erasure and virus-scanning at such a short notice?! We need to understand their predicament. A complete catch-22 situation!

Tail-Piece

Well, had it not been for the conservation of wildlife and the local self-styled *Bishnois* our street *Salmans* and stray *Saifs* would leave no *Chinkara* alive. But then, they will, at present, need large doses of *Cinkara,* especially when the mass-copying and other unfair means seem to have lost that *magic-mantra.* Bad luck!

33

RIGHT & LEFT

He came home quite late in the evening. He was told by his wife that few people had dropped in during the daytime. They had come to invite him to the colony meeting at the local mosque after sunset prayers. "The right one or the left one?" he asked his wife. She pointed towards right.

He lived in a colony where there were two grand mosques in the neighbourhood; one was situated on the right side of his home and the other on the left. Besides these two mosques, few other mosques also lied adjacent to his colony, and were barely at a walking distance from his home.

Without much eagerness, he went to attend the meeting at the mosque. The mosque, which was ancient, had developed some cracks in its parapets and had less space to accommodate more *nimazees* (worshippers). The meeting was about raising the funds to construct a new mosque after dismantling the old structure. Not all members of the colony had turned up for the meeting. Nonetheless, it was decided that a particular monthly amount shall be paid by every family, and further financial help would be sought from other people.

Just after a week, the work for constructing new mosque started. The volunteers erected some barriers on the main road next to the mosque in order to slow down the traffic. They had hired the public addressing system, some plastic chairs and a table covered with a green banner on which the name of Allah was beautifully inscribed. The volunteers, mostly young, alongwith some grey-haired elders were asking for donation on loudspeaker from the passersby. Addressing the people by the brand and colour of the vehicles they were driving, the volunteers rigorously shouted for the money. Pouring out numerous supplications, they tactfully stopped almost every passing vehicle and asked for donation, even if any vehicle had moved several times via that route.

Some of the volunteers also went for door to door collection around the colony, and even asked for money from the pedestrians. Somehow, the donations made it possible that the ground floor of the mosque is constructed.

Hardly a month had passed when he was informed by his wife that a group of people from the management of the mosque situated on left side of his home have left a contribution receipt at his home, which he has to shell out within two days.

Next day, he visited the mosque. On reaching there, he saw a huge gathering outside the mosque. On enquiring, he was told that the mosque was to be pulled down to built a new one. He caught sight of the billboard outside the mosque depicting the sketch of new mosque. It was an outline of a colossal construction project. He turned to one of the elderly members of the management and politely said, "This mosque was not that old. The repairs would have sufficed". The member didn't bother to respond but addressed the gathering crankily, "If we can spend so lavishly on our palatial houses, what is the logic in not dismantling the old mosque and reconstructing it in a big way?"

Being a humble dweller of the colony, he paid the decent amount and shoved away from the crowd, and moved towards home with a thoughtful poise. After few days, the volunteers of the same mosque also started collecting money on the main road. They did not stop there only; few of them used "credulous appeals" to coerce passersby to donate money. 'The success will surely come your way anytime today, if you donate generously' . . . so on and so forth. From every home to every shop in the locality, the fund-raising was done painstakingly.

In a kind of subtle *Maslaki Jung* (sect clash), the two mosques became the casualty. The bricks of bigots pulled them down in a way not to stand up again. For the mosque on the right side, all the raised funds got exhausted and the management failed to furnish the ground floor completely, not to speak of putting up the soaring storeys. As far as the mosque on the left, it could not even knock together the slab for the ground floor. The monthly contributions by the residents proved inadequate to build such massive mosques. The meager resources couldn't help.

With both the mosques in the locality being under irregular construction, their respective managements prepared temporary arrangements for prayers. As the winter approached, there were no heating arrangements in any of the two mosques. Both the mosques witnessed gradual decline in the gathering for congregational prayers.

He too left attending to mosque affairs, and preferred to offer prayers either at his workplace or home. Few months later, his wife once asked for the reason behind his changed attitude. He gave a sarcastic smile and said—

> *"I don't dream of a perfect mosque,*
> *only a few square inches of ground*
> *that will welcome my forehead . . ."*

Mohja Kahf

The wife couldn't fathom much but felt that he is not happy over the change.

34

STORY OF PEOPLE

"It is now just three months left for your delivery. Moreover, the doctor has advised you relative bed rest," he said to his wife. "I think you should now move to your parent's home till you deliver the baby", he added. "Shall I have to be at your home only when I am in good health?" the wife retorted. "What do you mean to say by 'your home'?" he said raucously. "I mean nothing. I just wanted to know that have I got the desired acceptance in this house, even after being a mother of two-year-old daughter"? she replied discreetly, taking a deep sigh and added, "By the way, home receives the person in all shades, well or unwell. Isn't it so?" Hearing this, the husband left the room fuming, "I don't want to enter into any argument. It is useless". The door bunged up.

She sat wordlessly on the bed, ruminating over the issue. Perhaps, her husband had failed to comprehend that his wife was a woman who symbolizes sacrifice and patience. She had already excelled with the highest level of forfeit and endurance by entering into wedlock, leaving all her nears and dears after thirty long years, just for him.

She knew that most of the women in Kashmir are born to conform with such kind of 'customary norm'. After a pause, she rang up her mother.

Few days later, she went to her mother's place alongwith her little daughter. The brother had come down to take her. Her coming meant a troubled package for her frail mother by means of frequent follow-ups, regular antenatal examinations and all terminal pregnancy precautions. And the mother put up all this lovingly for she knew what the mother of any married daughter has to bear to keep up her marital world!

One day, the dusk appeared quite depressing and with the gradual approach of night, the daughter complained of some increasing lower abdominal pain. She was rushed to maternity hospital where she was hurried away to the operation theatre. Her mother, who wore uncertain and despondent look, was anxiously waiting outside the theatre. The wellbeing of her doting daughter was the prime concern.

All of a sudden, the door of the operation theatre creaked and the doctor came out. The mother stood up from the waiting bench in the corridor and went speechless. Doctor looked into her eyes. There were unsaid queries drenched in them. "She has delivered a baby girl", doctor said. "How is she?" mother asked intensely. "She is fine, we will just hand her over to you", doctor answered cheerlessly. "No, I mean to say my daughter", mother reacted impulsively. "She has not recovered yet, but we are trying . . . ." doctor said. "I want to see her, doctor", mother interrupted distressingly. The doctor stood mute.

The daughter had developed some delivery related complications. The mother was down in the dumps. She gathered courage and went to see her inside the recovery room. She sat beside her, disconsolate and dejected. While she caressed her head, the daughter opened her eyes and looked towards her broken mother. She was too drained to speak anything. "God has blessed you with another daughter", the sobbing mother whispered in her ears. The condition of her daughter was deteriorating bit by bit. The dreams that she had weaved for her prosperous marital life seemed getting tangled. The void in the eyes of her daughter conveyed something cosmic but unfathomable.

Out of the blue, she started gasping. Pulse went feeble and her blood pressure was not recordable. Mother was helpless. She could do nothing but see her daughter breathing her last. Doctors tried to resuscitate her but all in vain and had nothing to say except 'we are sorry'. The fatal words pushed mother to the wall. For doctors, it was just another maternal mortality. But for the frail old mother, the apple of her eyes was lost. She was leaving behind two small kids, absolutely alone in the sea of good and bad people.

The most ill-fated moment for a mother was to mourn the death of her young daughter. Destiny neither allowed the neonate girl to see the face of her mother nor did it let the mother to feed her.

The daughter had left two small angels for her mother as a source of both joy and pain. Now the old granny wanted to live for them. She thought of re-living her daughter through her granddaughters. No sooner this feeling helped her to take respite from the untimely shock, fate had some more suffering in store for her. The father of two small daughters started claiming his inheritance right over them. From asking about the personal belongings of his deceased wife to counting and enquiring for the material things he had given to her, he began to severe his relations with his in-laws on various pretexts.

A few months passed away. He re-married. Though he had religiously pledged to take care of both of his daughters, the infant baby was adopted by one of his relatives whilst the elder one was forced to snap relations with her maternal grandparents. In the process, the innocent childhood of both girls was scotched heartlessly.

Feeble granny had no more hopes to live. The pain of separation was killing. She had lost not one but three daughters. Luck was cruel for the infant girl as well. She got separated from her mother first, then granny, and latter from her father and sister.

Kismet did not give chance to two little angles to know the meaning of motherhood. But the people of this world also did not give them chance to know the meaning of sisterhood. Small wonder, people play more merciless than destiny!

35

BROKEN HOMES, BROKEN BONDS

A flower swallowed by bud,
A nest
marauded by dwellers,
A garden
withered by leaves
Can thee imagine?
Incoherence of minds
malaise of hearts
false affection
selfish sympathy
in conjunction,
under one sky
Can thee imagine?
Eyes nonchalant
towards sight.
Entangled in cocoons
bonds of love
displaying apathy,
Blood turning thin

Can thee imagine?
Self and Self
I and I,
Give and take
Interest and loss
Trade of relations,
Diminishing sincerity
Can thee imagine?
Yea, here!
Where apple of eye
becomes
an eyesore.
Narrow outlets,
narrow inlets.
Chocked sentiments
estranged affinities—
all galore,
all gamble.

A journalist once visited the biggest old age home in one of the cities in Kerala and wrote: "I saw one old man gazing at a single beautiful bright flower amidst many on the ground. He was so engrossed with its beauty that he would smile at it and shake his head. I wanted to pat his back or rather peep in his heart to read the message of the flower, but I opted silence and stood just beside him. After few minutes I saw a tear rolling down his cheek. I was perplexed—was he happy or sad? What was the message from the flower that made him sink so deep in his thought? What did it remind him? Was he gazing at the flower or his own life? I looked at his eye they were burning red with agony and pain. He had just realized that his life is just like this bright flower. Many would come and glorify the new bloomed flower in the dawn, but after a day or two when its colours had withered to darkness and it cannot stand firm with its head held high, the same people would walk unnoticed without even heeding its cry." (Old Age Homes by blogger Sharon Supriya)

Back home, there is a story to narrate about *him* . . . The wrinkled face parched and frail like a fallen *Chinar* leaf in autumn that once looked green and glorious. Behind the old visage, there was more of him to see. Struggling between past and future, verve and sloth, triumphs and letdowns, warmth and seclusion—he was coldly looking at the bank draft he had received just now. The looking glass in the room was reflecting a somber image of things. Life was no longer so as he knew; it was now ending in lonesome misery.

The fond memories of his only son were distressing him inwardly. The son after getting married had left old parents and settled abroad. The monthly packet of cash from him was wounding the aged father's affection and pride. The walk down-the-memory-lane flashed a beautiful, radiant sight before him: Those little soft fingers that he used to hold and the blossoming innocent smiles he used to crave for; the every moment of love and care that he had showered on his darling son. The mistakes he had overlooked generously and the time he had given away abundantly. The whole life had gone in making his son what he was today. The tender devotion was simply unconditional and all-embracing but its memories were turning heart-rending now . . .

Dil Chu Pranain Kathan Sanaan Bazeh
At times, heart ponders over the past
Seeni Manz Naar-i-Kol Khanaan Bazeh
And burrows the stream of fire within

(Prof.Rehman Rahi)

The sick wife was just speechless. She had gone into dementia, forgetting where his son is and why he had deserted his parents so desolately. Both husband and wife had sacrificed and slogged all through their life for him, with a hope that a day would come when they will rejoice their old age with his support and caress, and all else will naturally appear cheerful.

However, it wasn't so. The blood had gone thinner and fast life had brought meanness in the relation. It was agonizingly unimaginable to see the son not sparing even a few moments for his lonely parents just because he was too engrossed in his wedded world, taking pleasure in the company of his 'modern-thinking' spouse. The young couple was getting self-centered, craving for a *separate space* for themselves. Values and principles of family life were alien to his other half. She had flaunted her tantrums around, pushing the hen-pecked hubby to the wall, gradually.

Living under one roof, the family was torn down emotionally. Sincerity in sharing and contributing for the home was vanishing as thought of building a 'mini world' took strong roots with each passing day. The gap was widening and mutual co-existence was getting unbearable.

Parents were surprised and shaken to notice the upsetting behavioural changes in their son. He wasn't like this before. They had taught him the best lessons of life. But then, the 'new ideals' had transformed his outlook. Priorities had undergone alteration. Obedience of parents, come what may, was now an impossible sermon for him. He wasn't ready to ignore and wink at the attitudinal flaws of his aged parents, forgetting how they forgave his every wrong since childhood. He had harshly stopped thinking about how they endured his imperfections, grooming him into a young man.

Eventually, there was a break-up. With an *alibi* of 'looking for greener pastures', he left his loving parents and sweet home for good. A monthly meager sum of money was the only link he had sustained with them for unknown reasons.

The parents were moving on with nobody there for them until few months when the ailing mother passed away. The son was informed but didn't turn up, just condoled his father over the phone. The tight schedule and stringent rules at his work place overseas were cited as the cause of his absence over his mother's funeral.

The lonesome father was now buried amidst books and newspapers, spending his twilight years in oblivion. There was no old age home around to shelter him and his solitude.

The hypocrisy of his society in acknowledging the social challenge he and his ilk face were brushed away casually. Sons didn't drop their parents at old age homes; they deserted them in their own hearths by their lackadaisical attitude and criminal apathy.

They almost become unwanted and a burden for them.

Time is a precious lifeline that they are holding back to them, and the same *Time* is running out of their hands as well.

It's all just a matter of time!

36

BEYOND THE VISIBLE

Even today I remember that disquieting day. My friend's grandpa was admitted in SKIMS for treatment and I had gone to see him. He was critically out of sorts and I was standing close to his bed, staring his shiny white-bearded face all eyes. There was a slight commotion around the other bed aside. I moved my head and caught the sight of the old lady patient who too had been in the ward for a couple of days.

She was dying and breathing her last. Her relatives and family members were huddled together near her, waiting for the final moment. The doctor examined her again for the umpteenth time but despair writ large on his face. He called one of her sons to explain the grim prognosis. He was a professor and his sister was a research fellow. They started conversing with the doctor while the rest exhibited blank looks, not comprehending what the talk was about. The doctor, who was young and seemed religious-minded, advised them to recite the Holy Qur'an as their mother's end was imminent. She was suffering from a chronic debilitating disease with multi-organ failure.

The family members began to search for the Holy Book but all in vain. At this odd hour, somehow a pocket sized Holy Quran was made available by a good Samaritan. But the surprise was yet to come. None of the family members including qualified son and daughter were able to read, not to speak of reciting the Holy Book. Finally it was left to a nearby villager who assiduously began reciting the verses. Then only, after a few minutes, the mother left for eternal abode. Her corpse was taken away amidst screams and cries. It was a sardonic scene. The blank expression of Mr Professor and Ms Research Fellow while their mother hit the trial was dismal.

In an unconscious reflex, my friend clasped the right hand of her grandpa firmly with her two palms. Her grandpa opened his eyes and whispered—"Dear, recite the last verses of *Surah Al-Baqarah*". She started the same, bowing herself down to the position of her grandpa. While tears rushed down her cheeks and her tongue stumbled, her father helped her to continue and soon the ailing old man also joined the recitation albeit at a low ebb.

After some days, he was shifted to intensive care unit following deterioration. Costly drugs and injections turned ineffective and renowned doctors gave up.

Eventually, he was moved to the ancestral home as per his last wish. All the next of kin gathered around the bed, and my friend was lying nearby rubbing the feet of her grandpa. His flaccid feet were getting colder and he was gasping. Amidst slow murmuring of *Kalimah* from the lips of everyone present, his elder son kept a level head and began the recitation of *Surah Yaseen*. The moment he uttered *'Salamun-Kowlun-Min-Rabin-Raheem'*, the old patient gradually closed his eyes, heaved a long breath and then . . . .

It was not a last sleep but the final awakening. To our Maker, we all shall be brought back, leaving the world which is the briefest of interludes in our never-ending life span. As a well spent day brings comfortable sleep, the well-used life brings a relieving departure. The old man had departed for another world in a way quite different from the old patient lady. It was a simple antithesis. The difference was discernible.

It is ironical that we know everything except what we should know best. Almighty, besides granting us with two eyes, has given us also a 'third eye' for scanning the invisible realities beyond the normal limits of human perception. And this third eye is the intellect. We remain in ignorance because most of us don't care to use this 'third eye'. We reckon that the total reality is what we can see with our two eyes. If only we were just to give the matter some earnest thought, we would become even more certain about what remains unseen than about what is visible.

Life is an intricate passage, and at every step there is a chance to decipher the meanings that are finer and subtle for consequential living moments. There is a need to transcend beyond the visible and comprehend the imperceptible.

37

FOR 1400 BUCKS!

It was cold and dark outside. Rain storms were lashing through the barren fields. Lightning and thunder really made one's teeth to sweat. Scared dogs were howling and aimlessly looking for a secure place to hide in. Fragile and arid standing trees had already shed their leaves. Amidst this air, was a standing small old shack. Mud walls of hovel barred nothing from coming in. However, the hay roof permitted everything to sneak in but a ray of hope and light.

Small girl in the hovel, while striving hard to prevent a kerosene lantern from quenching, suddenly heard a scream of her mother. Before she could gather herself and reach to her mom, she had fainted while feeding her youngest son. The frightened girl was just eleven years old, but happened to be the eldest of her other three sisters and two brothers. She had no one to lend a hand as her father was as usual out gaming with his acquaintances. The little girl had no option but to call out for help.

She managed to gather a few neighbours who took her mom on a cart to nearby road where from she was lifted in a bus to the town hospital. The little girl requested one of the neighbourhood ladies to stay back with her younger sisters and brothers. Before her mother could reach to the hospital, she actually gained some consciousness and complained of lower abdominal pain. While heading towards the hospital, the condition of her mom was gradually worsening.

Somehow, the bus managed to reach to the town hospital. Yet luck had no package for the little girl that night. They had to bash the main door of hospital loudly, till someone from inside the hospital came to open it. The attendants came to know that electricity of the hospital had snapped due to bad weather. The orderly in the hospital lit some candles and took the patient to the examination room and went to call the lady doctor on night duty.

"Oh no, she is the same lady!" the doctor exclaimed no sooner she saw the morose patient lying in stupor on the bed. "She is pregnant, her seventh one. I had already warned her", the lady doctor added. The desolate patient was merely in her late twenties and, in fact, was being checked and followed by the same lady doctor during previous pregnancies. After the birth of her sixth child, she was advised by the doctor to prevent any further conception apprehending certain pregnancy related complications in her. But the ill-fated lady had never imagined that her life would be put to stake for the meager sum of fourteen hundred rupees by her pitiless husband, who was a failure by all means. The poor little girl never knew that her mom was forced to conceive so that the little girl's worthless father would get 1400 rupees after the institutional delivery of his wife.

The night was getting darker and rains did not tend to stop. As it was cold, few scruffy and ragged red hospital blankets were put over the patient. "She is in a premature labour pain, shift her to labour room without more ado", the lady doctor said while examining the patient. After an arduous struggle, the orderly of the hospital someway succeeded in obtaining the keys of the labour room and lit the portable lighting gas that pertained to it. As there was no stretcher in the hospital, the poor lady was lifted by some of her neighbours and taken to labour room. The doctor rushed to the labour room and wore a pair of gloves. "The fetus is just in its eighth month, but it's too late to stop the progression of delivery now", doctor said hastily. She asked all the attendants with the patient to leave the labour room at once. The depressed little girl left, looking back constantly at the face of her mom.

The doctor opened the knot of a locker that was tied with a piece of dressing bandage and took out one steel box that contained some instruments used for the delivery of child. The illumination of the lighting gas was getting dimmer and it seemed that gas was running down. The doctor, by some means, delivered a skinny male baby with some signs of life. The nurse who assisted the doctor wrapped the baby in an ordinary sheet. There were signs of receding pain and grief on the face of mother while her baby was being delivered. "Doctor, the condition of baby is unwell; and we don't have electricity here, we could have otherwise put him under the heat lamp", said the nurse. "We need to refer the baby", replied the doctor while examining him. The doctor wasn't surprised to know that the hospital ambulance was out of order.

Just outside the labour room, the terrified little girl was sitting on a waiting bench. The night was stiffly drawing out for her. She was waiting for her mother to be taken home, staring persistently at the flame of flickering candle that was put at the end of the corridor near the window. The candle was the only source that emitted a little light in the long corridor.

"Doctor, blood pressure of the patient is non-recordable, the pulse is feeble as well", nurse shouted. The doctor, who was attending the baby, rushed to the patient. The doctor had already given all the possible medication to stop her bleeding, but all in vain. While feeling her pulse, the patient gripped her fingers around the hand of the doctor and looked towards her. The doctor was helpless, but fixed her eyes on the patient. She could read her teary eyes which had the will to live but couldn't; and which had the life but was dying so low-priced. For just 1400 bucks!

The doctor heard her gasping though she had tried her best to revive the patient. She watched her dying very cheap.

All of unexpected, the strong wind thrashed the window open in the corridor and drenched the candle near it. The anxious little girl who was sitting in the corridor was tersely swallowed up in total darkness.

COSMOS

38

Unforgettable Words

I learned a lesson at the age of 17 that I never forget . . . . One day the headmaster walked into the classroom, and he put up a broad white sheet of paper, about 1 metre by 1 metre, with a small black dot in the corner. And he asked—"Boys, what do you see?" And all of us shouted in unison—"A black dot!?" And he stood back and said—"So not a single one of you saw the broad white sheet of paper? Don't go through life with that attitude."

There couldn't be a more convincing anecdote on positive thinking and this universal edification came from none other than Kofi Annan, the former Secretary General of the UN who assumed the mantle of the topmost international civil servant on the dawn of 1997 and rose to this summit from the position of a minor official in WHO 35 years ago. He climbed every rung of the success ladder after going through with all and sundry concerned with every segment of UN—from budget, personnel, pensions, refugee affairs to diplomacy and the delicate balancing act of peace-keeping in theatres of conflicts.

Kofi Annan is one such dazzling example of men with a halo of achievement in the world of mediocrity. He remembered the golden words of his teacher which imbibed in him an unflinching spirit to strive and move ahead through thick and thin. Today, the lesson of his teacher marks him from the riff-raff and run-of-the-mill genre.

It is said that a teacher affects eternity, he can never tell where his influence stops. Indeed, it is a reality provided teacher is a 'teacher' in sincerity and faith. Each taught word of his becomes an unforgettable legend for the pupil.

I remember those nice days when I was a collegiate, and the maturity of life was slowly dawning on me with the succour of my teachers, especially the one who taught the English subject. She was a sober and erudite lady. She also had the privilege of being a member of National Commission for Women. I never missed her class. Once after finishing her lecture on Mathew Arnold's poem 'Dover Beach', she asked the whole class to jot down its summary. Incidentally, I was the first to do and show it to her. While she went through my text, she was smiling. I got nervous apprehending that I have probably blundered somewhere. However after going through my lines, she said—"Why haven't you gone in for literature?" I couldn't pop out a word for I was slightly confused. She asked further—"What after graduation?" I gathered my lost wits and vehemently told her that I was interested in journalism. "What?" she said sarcastically, "*Journalism Main Ja Kay*

Sach Likhna Hai! (You wanna write truth by joining journalism). I wish you could do so since anybody can get to truth but only a few can write it. Anyway, all the best". With this, she invited the attention of the whole class and read my text loudly. Though very small in importance, but it was a pristine pleasant moment. Unforgettable.

I wasn't aware as to where destiny will drag me. Today, I find myself in a tight spot. Truth is the motif of my profession, and shiftiness mars its sanctity. But I am unable to classify who is who. Who is *Anybody* and who are *A Few*—it seems to be an enigmatic question in the atmosphere full of uncertainty, scare and mistrust. And then, the way the powerful tool in my hand often loses power and vomits out trivia, it makes me realize that I have yet a lot to learn, yet a lot to go. And may be, this learning process will never end. The quest is both interesting and intriguing.

Writing truth is, of course, a *magnum opus*. It requires passion for the truth. It is indeed an uphill task and none can guarantee that the next step one takes is safe. But it is up to a person to make the best of his walk—if he stumbles, it is up to him to pick himself up and move forward, and not lie still and rot. Those who possess such passion, those dreams and convictions are shaped by it and not by their hurts—they alone leave foot prints on the sands of time and carve a niche for themselves. They are the pacesetters, others try to emulate them. Someone has rightly pointed out—"Example is not the main thing in influencing others, it is the only thing".

Further about my teacher, the destiny brought me in front of her again across the table. This time not alone but alongwith my three-year old kid who innocently spoke the truthful things when she conversed with him. My smiling teacher was looking ever-serene. And I was re-situating myself in a different search.

39

LIVING IN ROME . . .

Reason, logic and sense—the sane usage of these terms nowadays stirs the hornets' nest. People with chaotic brains get furious and jump to bite you. Talk rot but don't talk sense—this is the lesson they teach you. And then who doesn't know that in order to survive in Rome, one has not to fight but follow Romans! One has to vomit dirt in the manner others do through their foul mouth and pen. One has to behave like a gaga and act like a 'Moron'. One has to oblige every Mr. Simple Simon who happens to be the 'Head' of anything. One has to accomplish any wrong and justify the same through any nonsense. In brief, one has to do everything which everybody every time is seen doing in Rome—Yes, throttling the sacred essence and meaning of life, tarnishing the truth, and befooling others as well as one's own self.

"Turn a blind eye, dear, just be Blind" —these words of a friend console me whenever I see wolves turning amuck and lambs running for life; whenever I hear vehement barking of dogs and ludicrous stammer of sensible; and whenever I witness all that which smacks of corruption of thought, corruption of deed and corruption of cash all around.

Object, argue and dust the jacket, this is what some of us may wish to do with everyone who seems absolutely wrong but thinks he is absolutely Mr. Right. A renowned thinker once said, "There is nothing that helps a man in his conduct through life more than knowledge of his own characteristic weakness, which guarded against becomes his strength". Verily no soul on earth is impeccant but it doesn't mean that we allow slack tendencies of our nature to prevail on us and become a living weakness *per se*! Instead of fighting against suffering sickness, why to allow ourselves to be infected with more moral contagion?

The fact is that every person in world is not content with what he is or what he has. The pendulum of his insatiable desires always shows an upward swing. As such, he looks for outlets which can provide him a sort of solace, and in this 'pursuit' he eventually halts at inordinate full-stop since bad things/means are always more enrapturing and sapid. The whole process leads to pollution of every kind, passing from smoke into smother. Seeking happiness in satisfying the desires by way of ignoble ways vanquishes the method of seeking the happiness by limiting the desires. Bernard Shaw writes—"You have no right to consume happiness without producing it than to consume wealth without producing it."

The question arises: how to produce happiness? Well, happiness is a state of mind. You can simply produce and find it by being grateful to Almighty; by being comfortable with your conscience; by being with your good companions; or by being in love with those who love Almighty. Ironically, happiness has been a misnomer for most of us. We derive so-called happiness from pitiful things like dancing to the tunes of film lyrics, TV-watching, eating tasty food, donning gaudy clothes, wearing pompous ornaments and more so from owning a grand house and car. To be precise, happiness has been integrated with any sort of perversion and a plausible terminology has been invented to justify the same. We have been successful in maintaining a charade.

All the same, plugging the loopholes or flaws in any society or system or set-up is not altogether a chimera or a hopeless case. There is always a scope for rectification. Planet earth, hitherto, hasn't at all got filled with filthy souls in entirety! Noble souls and hearts still exist amongst us. And it is they alone for whose sake Almighty is still sustaining this world which otherwise appears ripe for a drastic doom.

Such souls aren't simply ordinary. They are extra-ordinary. Unlike many of us, they have the sound faculties to grasp the superficiality of this flimsy world, and the reality of life hereafter. They never mould the divine truth because of personal expediency. They speak it out boldly even if it goes against them. They counter their opponents by substantial arguments and not by jumbled street-jargon. Incoherence of words and deeds is not their hallmark. They known that world is not their perpetual abode, and that's why they live like travelers—unassuming, simple and selfless. For them—

> *Life's but a walking shadow,*
> *a poor player.*
> *That struts and frets his*
> *hour upon the stage*
> *And then is heard no more.*

(William Shakespeare)

But then, good men never die *ala* good deeds. We certainly hear about them ever and anon. They live in hearts and in history. And that's their victory.

40

LIFE'S LIKE THAT!

'I'm disgusted'. These words have become a cliché with one of my friends. Even as it seems that she possesses a breaking point of high magnitude, the very little things in life perturb her quickly. I don't know why. Her behavior always sets me thinking. She is not self-centered, it is for sure. However, she is not even self-contented. Her whimsical complexity lies somewhere in between this queer antithesis.

The fact remains that human being is an embodied paradox. Perhaps, a bundle of contradictions. Consistency never lasts. You go on creating or moulding yourself as per the demands of various situations in life. You are never what you really are. Life steadily moves on as an uncompromising reconciliation of uncompromising extremes. And you just casually call it 'adjustment'—a continuous process of adjustment. It cannot be otherwise. You have your choice. You can either accept different situations as inevitable or adjust yourself to them.

Else you can ruin your life with rebellion and you may end up with a nervous breakdown!

Then, this adjustment is never purely for the sake of self-seeking. There dawns a stage in everyone's life when one doesn't just live for one's own self alone. You live for others also, your parents, family and friends. And for them, your self-sacrificing becomes your self-adjustment. They hardly come to know how, for their sake, you relegate your selfhood to background. It is rather good to see them oblivious of this intangible feeling of yours, which underlies your self-motivation. Besides, your sensibility demands the silent and deep burial of sacrifices. Exposition means simply expiration when your sensibility aspires—

Koi Najaat Na Pae Najaat Sai Pehlay
Let none achieve 'salvation' before salvation

Bernard Shaw classified the two tragedies of life. One he said, is not to get your heart's desire; the other is to get it. In both cases, it infers that life is a tragedy. Even if it is so, it is not something mournful because tragedies are often the tools by which Almighty fashions us for better things. They may appear stumbling blocks in our way but ultimately they turn to be the stepping stones to a good life here and hereafter.

Of course, the more poignant sufferings are unforgettable. Life is really a general drama of pain. Nevertheless, disgust is not its denouncement. In one or the other way, trials and tribulations are the part of everyone's life. Everybody has a burden to bear. Painful disturbances in life are usually ephemeral. When the emotional inducement is exhausted, reason returns to its rightful position in the mental scheme. The power of reason in the mind of any individual during an emotional crisis, and the duration of the crisis, depends upon the extent of development achieved prior to such crisis. That's why some break quickly, some take time, and some don't break at all. For the latter—

Muqamat-e-Aah-o-Fughan Aur Bhi Hain . . .
There are other destinations as well

The development implies the spiritual one. And it alone is the real sense. This spiritual development is nothing but an unflinching faith in Providence. In the lexicon of faith, there is no such word called despair or disgust. What is disgusting for others is an intimation of the way of Almighty to a believer. This is the ultimate of spiritual development, when you practice resignation. Resignation is not meek withdrawal. It means putting Almighty between you and your troubles while keeping the quest on. Strive and struggle is the hallmark of such survival.

After all, what is to be shall be. Whatever will be, will be. Isn't life like that?

Tum Khaof-o-Khatar Se Dar Guzrow
Let you overcome fear
Jo Hona Hai So Hona Hai,
What is to be shall be
Gar Hasna Hai To Hasna Hai
Gar Rona Hai To Rona Hai
You will weep or smile
As destined

41

NEVER MIND!

Then of the Thee In Me who works behind
The Veil of universe, I cried to find
A lamp to guide me through Darkness, and
Something then said—
'An Understanding blind'

In the whirlpool of life, when without tends to dictate within, I often recall this beautiful quatrain of Omar Khayyam.

I am not a poet and as such can't subtly interpret the mystic connotations of Omar Khayyam's words. But it sounds that an understanding blind is a person who recognizes and perceives well the extent of his blindness. Although blind and no judge of colours, he realizes that he is groping in the dark and seeks light to lead him on the right track. In other words, he is a person who cannot see, but can listen to the "still small voice" within.

At certain junctures in life, a tormenting clash hits you. You feel you are wedged up unknown and your cherished notions are facing a threat. It seems as if you are getting drowned in the ocean of maddening crowd and the shore of your mind is drifting away. Even though your head makes you to adjust and fine-tune with the ambience, the inner person within you but seems angry and annoyed always. There is no other way perhaps. It resembles a sort of forced choice.

Recently I had a very long conversation with my best friend, my hubby. He quoted the saying that as the magnetic needle always points towards the North, hence it is that the sailing vessel does not lose her course. So long as the heart of man is directed towards Almighty, he cannot be lost and drowned in the ocean. He will definitely reach to the destined shore.

Obviously he wanted to convey that strong people are not nettled by adversity. They believe in the words that "there is nothing stable in human affairs, and therefore avoid undue elation in prosperity or undue depression in adversity". A balanced approach is quite necessary to give life a genuine meaning. There is every possibility of a new and perhaps a different kind of lesson dawning on you even amidst unfavorable circumstances. And as they say, alien ideas can be received like guests, in a friendly way, but with the reservation that they are not to tyrannize and transform their host.

How forcible are right words! When they knock on the door of heart, an echo is sure to come from within. A chord is struck somewhere in the soul. The clarity is so awe-inspiring that the listener is promptly convinced. Right words, even a few, are always bound to create righteousness.

Thanks to my friend whose offbeat views, good advice and proffered knowledge always comes to my rescue. His words have a magical effect. After listening to him, I always re-affirm my determination to go on through thick and thin.

The other day he narrated an interesting event related to a person who is hailed as one of the wisest men of all times: Socrates. The marital life of Socrates was miserable. His wife gave him hell. She regarded his strange attitudes and disdain for the temporal benefits as utterly foolish.

Once when she raved and screamed, Socrates chose not to respond. She tried her level best to draw him into an argument. However, she found him deaf to all her criticism. Her words failed to trigger him into a verbal joust. She became frustrated. She decided to make him respond in anyway. For this there was need for something more than mere words. Only then would Socrates realize the depth of her anger. So, she picked up a pot containing water and emptied its contents over his head. Socrates quietly rearranged his robes, ran his palm over his bald head, while mumbling—"After so much thunder, it is only reasonable to expect a shower".

Of course, heavy clouds in the sky are usually accompanied with thunder-clap. And they are best relieved by the letting of water ala heavy hearts. Things seem better after a good weep since tears are summer shower to the soul. But then only little minds get wounded by little things.

"Great minds never mind"—my friend uttered with aplomb.

42

A Brush with Beat Gen

The day was not that somber. However, it wasn't even placid. It was diversely dank. The cloudy sky and little drizzle made it sink poignantly in the inaccessible recesses of soul; the aching in the heart seemed to transmute into dinned moments, dissolving the inner thoughts in the vestige of outer world. I wasn't far from the madding crowd, and yet I felt a momentary liberation from an invisible status-quo. The rustic crowd around yokels enjoying their simpleton world: the excited hopes, false meanings, new dreams, long compliance, big promises, broken pledges, dramas, derisions, witlings, words, songs, screams—the confusion of the day got confounded in a whimper. I find myself stranded in a telephone booth, midway to home, as mobile towers were down.

Waiting eagerly for my turn to ring up home, informing about delay in getting back, I saw the evening beginning to descend on the horizon as half-visible sun almost dived beyond the mountain, passing the faint streaks of orange light from the curtains on fluffy clouds, as if emanating from a very mildly-burning crucible. The crows too cowed past in groups, saying good bye to yet another arduous odyssey. The ambiance was cool and full of sudden freshness as if a cry baby had fallen asleep after a daylong cajoling.

The scene through the glass panes of telephone booth was absorbing However, I failed to catch its total serenity. More than five minutes had whizzed and my urgent phone call still eluded me. Annoyed, I moved into the closet to request the loquacious caller to ring off early. The teen-age girl engrossed in a hush-hush call, was beguiling like a dim wit. The other girl besides her (probably a chummy) was also enjoying the long 'tele-talk'. The moment they noticed my presence, they stopped giggling and lapsed into embarrassed silence. We probably stood sizing each other up in the big mirror attached to the door of that dreadfully dark cubicle.

What they saw was me: an exhausted soul, past teens, who had taken the day off from loathsome monotony to accompany some social activists on a trip to an enlightened hamlet. And what I saw was too long haired blondes of about 16 or 17 in gaudy attire and several layers of make-up.

Unwittingly I had become their co-conspirator. Yet I was the enemy generation. Their look was hostile. Mine more unfriendly. But instantly I experienced a cooling-off period. Suddenly I wanted to take them in my arms. I wanted to wash the cheap make-up off their children faces. I wanted to shake them and beg— Don't do all this, go home!

Home? What did I known of their homes, I thought. Perhaps they were here because something was lacking at home. But I knew that if anybody in the world loved them enough to be concerned about their future happiness, it was the people in that imperfect place called *home.*

I wanted to attack the logic that seemed to assure the girls they were fleeing to something better. What did they hope to find: Love? Love in a foolish conversation, draining stink through the hard cables and gushing all dirt in a dead apparatus. Did they think this could make them feel more cherished? I felt jacked off.

I realized that the scene I was witnessing was a criticism of my generation, and a deserved one. We have permitted our young generation to be deceived by dazzling promises of a 'new' morality. We should have told them some bare truths, some hard dogmas, some vexatious but real facts. We didn't. We kept them in dark. We should have told them that even though marriage isn't perfect, it is the basic unit of our society and continues to be the best one that has been devised by nature and religion. We should have told them what is it that demarcates love from lust, trust from distrust or feeling from flirting.

The 'new' morality concept of letting instincts to be our guide, would be workable if human beings were merely animals—if we had no cognizance or soul. But man is more than animal and he debases himself when he lives on an animal level. Man is the highest of God's creatures. To surrender before his instincts and run like an alley cat is beneath his dignity. He is not what he has made of himself. There are treasures hidden in him, bounties of virtue lying dormant in his tumultuous soul. He is weak but he is not bad. And how can he be? He is a supreme creation of God, lovable, tameable. This is a decree of God which will never be changed by any words of feather-weight philosophers or by the scoffing of youthful rebels.

I wanted to tell the girls that, despite the bravado, when a young man marries he chooses a girl he can respect. This has been said many times to many generations of girls, but it is true today as ever.

I wanted to tell them that I could remember what it is like to be 16: the reckless impatience to get on with the business of living; the alternate ecstasy and agony of being young; the eagerness to love and be loved. At 16, one flirtatious chat is all-important. But I have lived some 20 years longer, and I have learnt that life is also made up of other equally, and sometimes even more important things: of sitting up with a sick, of holding the hand of the dying or of the bereaved, of smiling at hard buffets of fate, of weeping at losing something forever, of letting moments slip out from your fingers willingly, of sacrificing big issues of life for the smaller ones, and much, much more.

I may not have learnt things precisely but I have somehow assimilated that life is many splendored thing. The complete woman is more than a lover. She is a daughter, wife, mother, sister, friend, member of the community, citizen of her world. Her days and nights are woven together in a tapestry of joy, sorrow, success, failure, laughter and tears inherent in each of her roles. She cannot isolate one role than she can pull the tapestry apart without unraveling it.

I have found that every night eventually comes to an end, and then you have to face either the shining morn or else the cold, bleak dawn relapsing you back into direful dark night. This is perhaps the total realism of life. However, our teen-agers may brush it aside as a piffling. They claim to hate 'phoniness.' To some of them, the 'new freedom' sounds honest. Love, they say, is not to be shackled by rules and regulations; it should be spontaneous and genuine. However, this argument overlooks the fact that love without commitment is an impostor. And then, what love, affection, bond, relation, sincerity, or truthfulness actually means, is something that our beat generation is miserably ignoring to understand. Lacking proper education and guidance, they are living the way cookie crumbles for them. This or that way, they relish *Azaadi Dil Ki* and they boldly demand *Yeh Dil Maange More*.

I opened my mouth to say all this, but the girls had turned their backs on me. At that moment, I realized the true meaning of being absolute strangers: we were strangers travelling the same road, yet not seeing any of the same things. They belonged to my gender and yet we didn't belong to each other in any way. Our misunderstanding was colossal. They were afraid I would try to ruin their 'pleasing chat', their 'excited moments', their 'spree world'. They, however, didn't known that I was thinking of an apocalypse that can last a life time.

43

Spring is here

They say spring is the time and symbol of nature's rebirth. Of course, it is the season when nature stops weeping for gladness, clouds move, firmament gets clear, brightness radiates, flowers in garden blush with ease, pigeons coo and sparrows twitter in joy as they nest for their new nestlings. All this labour of love, and an exhilarating and invigorative ambience around makes the arrival of spring conspicuous. And that's perhaps why a lot has been said and written about *Aamad-i-Bahaar* (arrival of spring).

The other day while relishing the melodies of *ghazal* maestro Jagjit Singh, I was surprised when he sang ruefully—

Ab kay kis rang main aayi hai Bahaar,
In which colour has arrived spring this time?
Zard he zard hai,
Paydoon pae hara kuch bhi nahi
Trees are bearing no green but yellow

I took a quick dekko through the window glass pane and unexpectedly found delightful greenery outside. The small new leaflets on the boughs were giving the spectacle as if of a new life with new beginnings, new strivings and new endings. Who says it's pale and how can it ever be so—I asked myself and simultaneously felt pity for the lyricist who, I presume, had been bogged down deeply by melancholy, to the extent of impairing his sight. It is indeed ironical! The same 'irony' revives when our golden-voiced Vijay Malla of Kashmir sings tunefully—

> *Asi chhu dil-e-gulzaar dodmut,*
> Our garden of heart is ablaze
> *Shalmaarus keh karav,*
> What to do with 'Shalimar Garden'?
> *Yus ne shahlat pawe jigrus,*
> The spring that fails to solace
> *tath bahaarus keh karav.*
> What to do with such spring?

Now this is too much! Again it is the over-drawn sting of nuisance bug called *Melancholy*, which overshadows the verdant charm of spring season. Otherwise the human heart is virtually never set on fire and so never ever extinguished! A small pound of pulsating mortal flesh just what it is, unaware of large-sized platitudes and clichés attributed to it unjustifiably.

The fact is that unless a person lives with nature and transcends time, he cannot feel any change around him, he cannot take any interest in the

181

changing seasons. For him, every season is a season of agony, a season of pain. He laments over the past *ad nauseum* and heedless of the bounties that surround him, destroys his present foolishly. He looks for happiness in strangers' gardens while it grows unnoticed at his own fireside.

Spring season has nothing so special, nothing so exotic except its discernible arrival. Other seasons too come and then go. They too bring a ring of change in their own way. And they too have an intensity to capture our attention and make our lives appear as sweet as the murmur of the brook. If spring season is a feel-good season, then all seasons are spring seasons. As Faiz puts it—

> *Nahi hai koi bhi mausam,*
> There is no season
> *bahaar ka mausam*
> Other than spring

And it is just a matter of feeling. Just a one single feeling—a feeling of gladly accepting oneself as one is at present, without the add-on of dead yesterdays and unborn tomorrows.

What the Nightingale of India, Sarojini Naidu, said about spring season is something grandly remarkable and contemplative. She wrote—"Spring time has no date. It does not confine itself to the flowering of trees and singing of birds, it depends upon the attitude to life and the approach to life".

Yes, it is an undisputed reality that a sense of well-being and a sense of happiness is, in fact, a state of mind. A seemingly sickening view of surroundings can become charming, and with routine indifference chirpy birds and spring flowers could look unattractive. It all depends upon approach towards life. But all of us, unfortunately, dream of some magical and extra-ordinary rose-garden beyond our reach, instead of enjoying the narcissus and hyacinth that are blooming outside our windows today. How strange that we don't relish this little possession of life. How tragic fools we are!

Even up the creek, there is no go-off with life but a reason to live, a reason to fight back boldly, a reason to frustrate the cheap designs of our rivals, a reason to see ourselves on right path, and all this with a reason to spend and fill fleeting moments of life with scintillation and symphony as of the spring air; to remain afloat on the cloud nine always, craving and aiming for lots of ameliorative greening, both in our lives and in our surroundings.

All we have to do is feel life around us. And when it is spring time, you don't have to feel it. It comes to you itself with a new spark of life. As Allama Iqbal said it so many decades ago—

Phir baad-i-bahaar aaye,
The spring breeze is flowing again
Iqbal ghazal khwan ho
Start singing, O Iqbal
Ghuncha hai agar gul ho,
If you are a bud be the flower,
Gul hai tow gulistan ho
If a flower the garden become

44

'I WAS SAFE SO LONG AS . . . .'

Graham Greene, the British author, wrote in one of his memoirs titled 'Ways of Escape' (1980) that "Writing is a form of therapy; sometimes I wonder how all those who do not write, compose or paint can manage to escape the madness, melancholia, the panic fear which is inherent in the human situation."

Of course, there is an element of lunacy and wretchedness embedded in each aspect of human life which at times becomes frightful to face and battle out. And any creative work just chips in to help us cope up with the whole drama. It also opens up interestingly novel and unexplored vistas of understanding related to any particular situation.

Going back to Greene, he in one of his narrative from the essay 'The Lost Childhood' recounts the precarious instant when he first discovered that he could read. He writes—"I remember distinctly the suddenness with which a key turned in a lock and I found I could read—not just the sentences in a reading book with the syllables coupled like railway carriages, but a real book . . . . All a long summer holiday I kept my secret, as I believed: I did not want anybody to know that I could read. I suppose I half consciously realized even then that this was the dangerous moment. I was safe so long as I could not read—the wheels had not begun to turn, but now the future stood around on bookshelves everywhere waiting for the child to choose—the life of a chartered accountant perhaps, a colonial civil servant, a planter in China, a steady job in a bank, happiness and misery, eventually one particular form of death, for surely we choose our death much as we choose our job. It grows out of our acts and our evasions, out of our fears and out of our moments of courage . . . ."

Many of us have speckled experiences whenever we confront a new happening, a new episode, a new situation in our daily lives. There are some unusual truths and realities that one gets familiar with often, and is astonished at the atypical enigma that gets unfolded in the process.

The inscrutability of human life and its formless facets will perhaps make most of us to moan in the tone of Graham Greene like this:

'I was safe so long as I could not come out of my mom's womb to breathe in the mysterious world;

I was safe so long as I could not make out what is what to judge the insignia of the life;

I was safe so long as I could not guess who is who to form an opinion about others;

I was safe so long as I could not think about the intricacies of human behaviour;

I was safe so long as I could not believe that even human brains can be shady;

I was safe so long as I could not imagine that sincerity can be termed suspicious;

I was safe so long as I could not infer that blood is actually thinner than water;

I was safe so long as I could not assume that friends can be foes;

I was safe so long as I could not be happy;

I was safe so long as I could not be successful;

I was safe so long as I could not trust my susceptible students;

I was safe so long as I could not compete with my brittle teachers;

I was safe so long as I could not demur against my big-headed boss;

I was safe so long as I could not be a fanciful rebel;

I was safe so long as I could not question the questionable;

I was safe so long as I could not see what I am seeing;

I was safe so long as I could not listen to what I am listening;

I was safe so long as I could not read what I am reading;

I was safe so long as I could not write what I am writing;

I was safe so long as I could not murmur a word;

I was safe so long as I could not sing what I am singing;

I was safe so long as I could not close my eyes and feel that bad people

have a bad end and world will be a lovely
location to live in;
  I was safe so long as I could not dream;
  I was safe so long as I could not think;
  I was safe so long as I could not hope;
  I was safe so long as I could not be understood;
  And I was safe so long as I could not believe I am I!

Now that I am unsafe, I cherish the bliss of ignorance, the moments of unawareness that were so calming and comforting, de-making the world a bad, brute place.

I am vulnerable, now. From every corner. I am scared. I am snared. The claws of injustice and unfairness, crooked and criminal, mean and malicious can pounce on me anytime. Perhaps on anyone, around. That's why some of us have already 'Lost the World' ala Graham's childhood.

45

A Cigar, A Cry

I always wondered why men smoke. To be frank, I had a strong revulsion for smokers. But only yesterday, my antipathy and curiosity was resolved. More precisely, it was dissolved! After a pretty long time, I ventured into my library for a dusting. As I wiped off the dusty racks, a small book slipped out. The prologue opened with the saying of Edward Bulwer: "A good cigar is as great a comfort to a man as a good cry to a woman."

That's it! Without going through the rest of book, I committed the adage to memory and made it food for thought for the rest of leisure time.

Men usually don't weep. But those who do, they are ridiculed as 'sissies', thought to be lachrymose or not to be is no criterion for measuring cowardice or boldness.

In fact, it is not in the sublime nature of man to shed tears or split hair in an hour of crisis. Even as he is troubled on every side, he doesn't look destroyed.

He may be persecuted or cast down, yet he never looks entirely forsaken or distressed. He adroitly keeps the appearances. That is why he is called Man—the one who has the power to will.

Nevertheless, human nature has a tendency to look for outlets lest one should burst like a cloud. Man, in order to alleviate his pain, resorts to ways other than crying. Majority of men smoke simply because they get a psychological relief although smoking is no panacea at all for anything. It is deleterious to health and shatters families beyond any doubt. It can never allay the pain or stand as a moral support in wilderness. Perhaps except one's own self, no one else sincerely shares anybody's burden, not to speak of mere two-inch tobacco filled coffin nail.

In spite of this lucid logic, men continue to vent their agonies and discontent in a puff of smoke . . .

Har Fikhr Ko Duwain Main Udta Chala Gaya . . . .

They can't cry, that's why they smoke. Perhaps they fail to comprehend that if they can't cry, they can try harbouring *Faith* that happens to be not just prevention but cure for all physical and mental ailments.

And then, there is a growing population of our youngsters who take to smoking just as a fad which gradually turns chronic. At times, it drags them even to worst types of addiction. An independent study reveals that be it a way to fight personal crisis, means to wipe the mental scars or just a sign of being cool, the youth in Kashmir have fallen into the net of drugs, with such cases increasing by 35-40% in the last few years. It further reports that 30-35% youngsters (15-35yr) have become victim of drug abuse (*Daily News and Analysis—25 June, 2010*).

Apart from the common causes of growing menace of substance abuse, one of the most important reasons of drug addiction in teenagers is probably communication breakdown. On home front parents fail to observe the behavioural changes in their children due to paucity of time, and even tend to compensate their absence with money. On societal level, the preachers have also fallen short to dispose off their duties in an effective way. The State institutions are pre-occupied with law and order issues, and have no priority to combat drug trafficking. Thus, the fatal menace.

Coming back to expression, there is certainly a communicative difference between men and women. Manliness and feminity are two different terms and they can't be incorporated in one being. Women have their ways. They are sensitive by nature and are more emotional than men—the fact substantiated even by modern research. Women know less but understand more since with them the heart argues, not the mind. Whenever a calamity or misfortune befalls them, they stagger quickly. Letting of tears is their only antidote to sorrow because after a good cry, things appear better.

Albeit women are good talkers and they candidly narrate their woes to every tolerant Tom, Dick and Harry—a good cry is still something indispensable. Tears soothe the curt twinge of psyche and pacify the sentiments. And at times, can create a difference provided these trickle down out of pious thought . . .

Aah Jati Hain Falak Pay Rahem Lanay Kay Liya . . .

No doubt women can smoke (and some even do) but they ought not to. A good cry is far better than a good cigar. A puff of smoke diffuses quickly in the thin air but a poignant cry from the bottom of heart can move the skies. Yes, that which is not allotted in destiny, the hand cannot reach and what is allotted, one can find wherever one may be—but 'dutiful drops' can make the find less wistful and the results fair.

46

GIVE ME A ROAD TO TRAVEL

I am not shocked. I am not even amused. I am just wondering. Looking for an answer. The morning clock is ticking fast. The countdown has begun. I have to leave before it's too late. I am rounding up my belongings. Unease is gripping me. The dilemma is very disturbing. I know the destination. But I don't have a road to traverse.

My four-wheeler is set for a strange journey. The jolts and jerks have already taken its toll. I can hear only thumps and thuds. The bumpy way has no sign of end. Dust and diversion blurs the voyage. And it all blurs me as well.

I encounter big monstrous machines, growling up soil from deep, making mounds as muddy artifacts. I see scattered pipes and people. The scene accompanies my cruise. There is no road in sight. I am moving along grimy path, in dilapidated lanes and by-lanes. The narrow lanes choke me for hours. My fuel is burning. My head is blazing. The honking horns are irksome. I can't budge. A scratch here, a collision there. I am just frightened. What a journey!

The cycle continues all through the year. The clock is pointing. I am a late-comer now. My journey is delayed forever. I am still in search of a road: A walk-able, a motor-able, a sustainable road.

Perhaps, roads here are never finished. For if they finish, many of us will finish too. The Industry of Roads will be shut down. The show makers will peter out. Our surplus money will go. Our irrelevant jobs will walk off. The plans will flop. The projects will fail. The dust will depart us. The men on work will disappear. Everything will change. And that we don't really want to!

So, I imagine travelling in vast sky, with no brutally mutilated macadamized thoroughfares, no traffic congestion. No descending poles, no hanging wires. The blue breezy highway will glide me to my destination. The white fluffy clouds will soak up the smog. In a twinkling, I will reach to my end. And I won't carry the hangover of tussled morning all day along.

Additionally, I will relish the bird's view from above. I will see people grappling over traffic jams, machines pulling out intestines of deceased roads, and men watching the spectacle with utter frailty. And, interestingly, I won't be the one down there, gazing at the situation so awkwardly. I will sing fusion in the skies:

Give me a road,
Give me a way,
I wanna trek along once again . . .

Give me a dream,
Give me a destination,
I wanna live up once again . . .
Give me a vision,
Give me a hope,
I wanna take up
my voyage once again.

My imagination breaks down. My wings can't take this flight. I am back in my world. The actual world where quality of life is getting inferior and life itself is becoming shoddier. I wonder how we live. How we *actually* go on living?! No sane soul will tolerate this torment. Is life lived this way? Can men of meaningful nation afford frittering away their time in finding roads to reach their places? What a tragedy!

Not only this, even our bigger issues face the same fate. We don't have roadmaps for anything at all. We are born to waste our time, waste our resources and waste our energies just this way.

There is no hope. There can be no bon voyage.